Heartland

One Day You'll Know

Heartland

Share every moment . . .

Coming Home

After the Storm

Breaking Free

Taking Chances

Come What May

One Day You'll Know

Heartland

❦

One Day You'll Know

by Lauren Brooke

SCHOLASTIC INC.

New York Toronto London Auckland Sydney
Mexico City New Delhi Hong Kong Buenos Aires

No part of this publication may be reproduced in whole or in part, or stored in a retrieval system, or transmitted in any form or by any means, electronic, mechanical, photocopying, recording, or otherwise, without written permission of the publisher. For information regarding permission, write to Scholastic Inc., Attention: Permissions Department, 557 Broadway, New York, NY 10012.

Library of Congress Cataloging-in-Publication data available.

ISBN 0-439-13035-2

Heartland series created by Working Partners Ltd., London.

Copyright © 2001 by Working Partners Ltd.
Published by Scholastic Inc. All rights reserved.

SCHOLASTIC and associated logos are trademarks and/or registered trademarks of Scholastic Inc. HEARTLAND is a trademark and/or registered trademark of Working Partners Ltd.

24 23 22 21 20 19 18 17 16 15 14 13   6/0

Printed in the U.S.A.
First Scholastic printing, September 2001   40

To Mary Ritchie — a wonderful friend who listens with her heart, not just her ears — just like Amy

Heartland

❧

One Day You'll Know

Chapter One

"Easy now," Amy Fleming murmured to Melody as the mare pulled against the lead line and whinnied restlessly to her foal. Unaware of Melody's concern, Daybreak, the four-day-old filly, trotted inquisitively around the field, her arched neck and intelligent head held high, her tiny hooves flicking lightly over the snow-covered grass. The pale November sun shone down on her bright chestnut coat. *It was a perfect Thanksgiving day....*

Amy held back her thoughts. No, she didn't want to think about it being Thanksgiving. That's why she was out here with Melody and Daybreak instead of in the farmhouse with Grandpa and her older sister, Lou. That's why she'd been working nonstop in the barn all day. She didn't want to think about it being her first Thanksgiving without Mom.

Melody whinnied again.

"It's OK, girl," Amy said, her fingers moving in light circles on Melody's neck. "Your baby's safe. She's just taking a look around."

Registering the familiar, comforting touch of Amy's hands, Melody turned her head. Amy rubbed the mare's forehead and felt her relax slightly and nuzzle Amy's arm. *If you're here,* Melody seemed to be saying, *then everything must be OK.*

A warm glow spread through Amy as she saw the trust in the mare's eyes. Only a month ago it had all been so different. When Melody had first arrived at Heartland, the horse sanctuary founded by Amy's mother, she had been exceptionally wary. But gradually Melody had overcome her nervousness and had grown to trust Amy. And since Amy assisted at Daybreak's birth, the bond between them had seemed to deepen further.

An icy breeze blew Amy's long light-brown hair across her face. She pushed it back, her gray eyes moving toward the little foal. Every step the filly took looked so full of energy; it was hard to believe that just a few days ago they had feared for her life. Her birth had been difficult, and for a while it had looked as if both the mare and foal might die. However, Amy, Lou, and Jack, their grandpa, had refused to give up, and at long last, as the stressful night gave way to morning, Daybreak had been born.

The filly stopped, her nostrils quivering, her beautiful proud head held high. As the rays of sun caught her coat, each chestnut hair seemed to flame brightly, but then the moment broke. With a toss of her head, Daybreak swung around. Cantering across the grass, she butted her head hungrily underneath her mother's belly and began to drink.

Amy watched her short, fluffy tail flicking from side to side and smiled. Ever since Daybreak's birth, she had felt an intense connection with the little foal. She wondered if it was just because she had been there at the filly's birth or whether it was something more than that. Her mom's voice came back to her: *Every so often a special horse will come along — a horse that will touch your life forever.* Looking at Daybreak, Amy was sure she knew what her mom had meant.

"Here, Daybreak," Amy murmured as the foal finished feeding. Daybreak took a step forward and sniffed Amy's outstretched hand, her intelligent eyes bright. "Good girl," Amy said softly, reaching to pat her neck.

With a squeal, Daybreak wheeled around. Amy jumped back just in time, gasping as the spirited filly kicked her back hooves feistily into the air and cantered off.

A voice hailed Amy. "Looks like she's going to be a handful."

Amy swung around. Scott Trewin, the local equine vet, was standing at the gate with Lou.

"Scott!" she exclaimed. "What are you doing here?"

"Oh, that's nice," Scott teased. "It's good to see you too, Amy."

"I didn't mean it like that," Amy grinned, going over. "I just thought you'd be at home, with it being" — she struggled with the word, "Thanksgiving and all."

"He just stopped by to wish us a happy holiday," Lou said, turning to smile at Scott.

He took her hand and smiled back down at her. "Well, I couldn't *not* see you, could I?"

For a moment Amy thought they were going to kiss. "OK — enough already," she said hurriedly. Scott and Lou had recently started dating, and although she was thrilled about it, there was a limit to how much she could stand!

Scott and Lou pulled apart, Scott grinning, Lou inspecting the tassels on her scarf. "So . . . how's Daybreak today?" Lou asked Amy, her embarrassment accentuating her English accent.

"Crazy," Amy replied, thinking, not for the first time, about how different she and her sister sounded. While Lou had lived nearly all her life in England, Amy had moved to Virginia when she was three. "But then she always is."

Lou smiled. "Well, Grandpa said to tell you everything will be ready in half an hour, Amy."

Amy felt her stomach contract at the thought of

Thanksgiving without Mom. "But there's these two to bring in and the back stalls to be mucked out," she appealed, "and the feeds to do. There's no way I can be ready in half an hour. Maybe you and Grandpa should go ahead and eat without me."

"Amy." Lou's voice interrupted her. Her cornflower-blue stare was sympathetic but firm. "You know Grandpa's put a lot of effort into this dinner. We all have to eat it together — that's the point. We'll give you a hand with the horses, won't we, Scott?"

"Sure." Scott nodded.

Amy's throat felt dry, but she knew that Lou was right. "OK," she said, fighting to keep her voice steady. "If you open the gate, I'll lead Melody in. Daybreak should follow."

However, when Amy led Melody out of the field, Daybreak stayed stubbornly where she was. Having tasted freedom for the first time, she seemed reluctant to give it up. Melody whinnied anxiously to her. Daybreak's eyes flickered from the field to her mother.

Scott stepped into the field, headed toward the foal. "Go on," he said encouragingly.

With a pert toss of her head, the filly put her ears back and cantered after Melody. Reaching the mare, she nipped her flank sharply as if to scold her mother for leaving her.

"Hey!" Amy protested. Flattening her ears, Daybreak

gave Amy a threatening glare, but Amy simply laughed and pushed her away. "You're going to have to learn some manners, baby," she told the foal. Daybreak looked at her haughtily, and Amy was reminded of Scott's earlier words. Daybreak was going to be a handful — no doubt about that.

❧

After Melody and Daybreak had been settled in their stall in the back barn and the final stalls had been cleaned, Scott left for his family's Thanksgiving. Amy watched from the stone-flagged feed room as Lou walked across the yard with him. Stopping by his car, they kissed. Lou watched until the vehicle disappeared out of sight and then came back toward the barn, a dreamy smile playing at the corners of her mouth.

"What do you want me to do?" Lou asked as she entered the feed room.

"Can you add some cod liver oil to those buckets and then mix them?" Amy said, pointing to a pile of feeds she had made up earlier.

Her sister nodded absentmindedly. "OK." She looked out the door again and then turned back to Amy, frowning. "What did you just say?"

"Lou!" Amy exclaimed. At twenty-three, Lou might be eight years older than Amy, but at that moment it felt like the other way around. Amy picked up the dusty cod liver oil can and put it into her sister's hands. "Cod liver oil — in buckets — then mix." She grinned as she propelled her normally sensible sister toward her task.

Lou started to pour dollops of the oil into the horses' food. "Scott's invited me to a Christmas reunion dinner in three weeks," she said breathlessly. "It's for all the vets in his year at college. It's black tie, so I'll have to find something formal to wear. Will you come shopping with me next week?"

"Sure," Amy said, starting to stir the feeds. She never had time to do much clothes shopping for herself, but helping Lou buy a gorgeous dress might be fun.

"I was thinking, you and Matt should get together," Lou said. "Then we could all go out on a date."

"Well, it's not going to happen," Amy said, thinking of Scott's younger brother, Matt. He was one of her best friends, and he'd been trying to get her to go out with him for ages.

"Why not?" Lou said. "Scott says Matt really likes you."

"Yeah, and I like him," Amy said. "But not like *that*."

"So who do you like?" Lou said.

Amy shrugged and started to pile the feeds up. "No one." It was the truth. There wasn't anyone at school that she wanted to date. *And probably just as well,* she thought. With winter setting in, there was always so much to do in the yard. Up at six o'clock every morning, she rarely stopped before midnight. The only boys she ever saw outside school hours were Heartland's two stable hands, Ty and Ben. For a moment an image of quiet, dark-haired Ty rose in her mind. She blushed as she remembered a day way back in the summer when he had touched her cheek and a shock like fire had run through her veins.

Lou obviously saw the blush. "Amy?" she said in delight. "There *is* someone, isn't there? Who is it?"

"There isn't anyone," Amy said quickly, pushing Ty out of her mind. She was being dumb. Ty was like a brother and best friend to her, not a boyfriend. "There really isn't." She grabbed the pile of feeds. "I'll go and hand these out," she said, hastily leaving the feed room before Lou could question her more.

The two sisters were rinsing the buckets by the water tap when the back door of the farmhouse opened and the tall figure of Jack Bartlett, their grandpa, appeared.

"Almost finished?" he yelled, his deep voice trailing across the yard. Suddenly, his upright shoulders jerked forward and he coughed heavily.

Amy frowned. "Are you OK, Grandpa?"

Jack cleared his throat as he walked toward them. "It's just a bad cold," he said, nodding. "I guess I picked

it up the other night when we were foaling Daybreak."
He changed the subject. "Now, are you coming in? Dinner's ready."

"We're coming," Lou replied.

As Grandpa turned back into the house, Lou gently took the water bucket from Amy. "Come on, Amy," she said. "It's time to eat."

Amy took a deep breath and followed Lou down to the back door. *It's going to be all right,* she told herself. She looked at Lou. Her sister appeared so composed; it was almost as though she didn't care that this was their first Thanksgiving since Mom had died. But Amy knew her sister better than that. Lou cared as deeply as she did. It was just that she had a different way of coping. Lou channeled all of her energy into being practical and sensible.

Reaching the porch, Amy pulled off her boots as Lou opened the door into the warm, brightly lit, cluttered kitchen. Grandpa was lifting a perfectly golden roasted turkey out of the oven.

"It all smells delicious, Grandpa," Lou said, going over to the sink to wash her hands. "Can I do anything to help?"

Amy stopped in the doorway, her heart pounding. Everything looked so familiar — the white candles on the table, the huge pumpkin pie cooling on the counter, the dishes of homemade cranberry sauce, sweet potatoes, and chestnut stuffing. As her eyes fell on the place settings, she tried to hold back the tears. At the far end of the table, where Mom had always sat, the tablecloth was bare.

Lou and Grandpa turned around at the sound of her crying.

Grandpa, his face creased in concern, put down the turkey and hurried over.

As his arms folded around her, Amy felt the grief that she'd been controlling so well during the last few months overwhelm her. She remembered so clearly the day when she had persuaded her mom to take the trailer out to lonely Clairdale Ridge to rescue Spartan, a half-starved stallion. She also remembered the storm and the tree falling, then waking up in the hospital and Lou telling her the news. Mom was dead.

She didn't know how long she cried, but at last she became aware of the room again and of the rough wool of her grandpa's sweater prickling her face.

"I'm sorry," she muttered, pulling back and trying to regain some control over her feelings.

"It's OK, honey — it's natural," her grandpa said. "Times like these are never easy when we've lost someone we love."

Amy looked into his blue eyes and saw the understanding there. "I miss her, Grandpa. So much . . ." she whispered, her heart clenching with loss. "And it's not just today, it's every day."

Grandpa kissed her hair. "We all miss your mom. We always will. But we've got each other, and today of all days we need to give thanks for that. It's what your mom would have wanted. You know how much she believed in looking forward to the future, not back at the past."

Lou rubbed Amy's arm. "Grandpa's right, Amy."

Amy swallowed and nodded.

"Come on," Grandpa said, hugging her one more time. "Let's eat."

The atmosphere around the table was subdued as they sat down. "I wonder what Daddy's doing right now?" Lou said, breaking the silence as they began to pass around the hot vegetable dishes.

Amy glanced quickly at Grandpa. His face had tightened. "Probably nothing special," she said quickly. "They don't have Thanksgiving in England, do they?"

"No," Lou admitted. "But he might be thinking of us."

"I'm sure he is, sweetheart," Grandpa said, only his taut mouth betraying his feelings. Amy knew Grandpa had never forgiven Tim, their father, for abandoning them and their mom after a riding accident had ended his international show-jumping career twelve years ago.

"I hope he got my last letter," Lou said, referring to the one she had put in the mail the previous week. "I asked him to call us today."

"Well, maybe he will," Grandpa said.

Sensing the awkwardness, Amy hurriedly looked at her grandpa. "We haven't said thank you for the horses yet," she said, blurting out the first thing she could think of to change the subject. "Mom always used to. We should, too."

Grandpa nodded. "You're right." He stood up and took down a thick, dusty photograph album from its place on the top shelf of the chest. He offered it to Amy. "Would you like to?"

Amy hesitated for a moment. She hadn't really thought beyond the need to divert the conversation from Daddy. "Oh," she said slowly. She took the heavy leather book and opened it, swallowing a lump in her throat. Page after page was filled with photographs of horses they had treated at Heartland. Amy looked inside the front cover and saw her mom's familiar writing: *By healing, we heal ourselves.*

"If you don't want to . . ." Grandpa began, looking at her face in concern.

"No," Amy said. "I want to." And suddenly she meant it. "Mom often told me how privileged she was, being able to work with the horses, and, well, I feel the same," Amy said, thinking of all the horses *she* had helped in the five months since her mom had died — Sugarfoot, Spartan, Promise, Melody. Glancing up at Lou and

Grandpa, she continued, "Every Thanksgiving, Mom said that by healing, we heal ourselves, and it's true. The horses I've helped have given me so much, and so I'd like to give thanks to them, just like Mom would have done."

Grandpa lifted his glass. "To the horses," he said. "To those in the past, the present, and those still to come."

"To the horses," Amy and Lou echoed quietly.

They put their glasses down and picked up their knives and forks. They had been eating in silence for a few minutes when Amy glanced across at her sister. Lou was looking at the photograph album, her eyes shadowed. "I wish I could have been here to hear Mom say those words," she said sadly.

Grandpa looked at her sympathetically. "You were never able to get off work, Lou."

"No," Lou said slowly. "I suppose I wasn't."

When they had finally finished eating the pumpkin pie, Amy and Lou cleared away the dishes and plates and then they all settled down in front of the TV for the evening. Around ten o'clock, Amy glanced at her watch. "I'd better go and check on the horses," she said, standing up.

As Grandpa stood up, he started to cough. "Do you want a hand?"

Before Amy could reply, Lou jumped to her feet. "You don't sound very good, Grandpa. You should stay in here where it's warm. I'll help."

After pulling on their jackets and boots, the girls went outside into the frosty night air. Lou seemed unusually subdued as they went around the stalls, collecting the empty hay nets and checking the water buckets and blankets. Amy looked at her sister and wondered what was on her mind.

When they'd finished, Lou went over to Sugarfoot's stall, and leaning against the stall door, sighed. "I wish I'd been here for at least one Thanksgiving with Mom."

Amy felt awkward. "You were always too busy. It was hard for you to come to Heartland, Lou."

"I could have come," Lou said. "I didn't really have to work every holiday."

"Mom understood how you felt," Amy told her. "She knew that the horses reminded you too much of Daddy and that it was easier for you to stay away."

"That doesn't seem like a good enough excuse anymore. I should have come." Lou stretched out her hand to stroke the little Shetland. "I should have made the effort. I didn't, and now —" She paused and looked down. "Now, it's too late."

Amy squeezed her arm.

Lou turned. "I missed out on really getting to know

one parent. I'm not going to make the same mistake again."

Unease stirred through Amy. "What do you mean?"

"Daddy," Lou said. "I can't stop thinking about him. I'm going to find him, Amy. I don't care what I have to do."

Chapter Two

That night, Amy thought about what Lou had said as she tried to fall asleep. Amy had been just three years old when Daddy had left and she had no real memories of him, except for the photos her mom had kept of him riding his horse, Pegasus. After the accident, she and her mom had left England to live with Grandpa in Virginia, while Lou, convinced that Daddy would one day return, had begged to continue going to her English boarding school. It was a hard decision, but their mom, reluctant to upset Lou any more, had agreed to let her stay. On Lou's rare visits to Heartland, she made no secret of the fact that she thought Mom and Amy had been wrong to leave England.

Shortly after their mom's death, Amy and Lou had

discovered a letter sent by their father to their mom five years before, begging for a reconciliation. Marion had never replied, but, determined to find their father, Lou had written to the address on the letterhead asking if they could arrange a meeting.

Amy hugged her knees to her chest and tried to imagine what it would be like to meet her father. Three weeks ago she had caught a fleeting glimpse of him at her mom's grave, but she hadn't realized who he was. It was only later that Grandpa had admitted that their father had visited Heartland earlier that day and Grandpa had refused to let him see his daughters. For a while Amy had thought that Lou would never forgive Grandpa, but eventually, on the night of Daybreak's birth, the two had made their peace.

Amy sighed. What would happen if Daddy *did* come back into their lives? After her mom's death, everything had been turned upside down — Lou had come back from her big job in Manhattan, and Ty and Amy had learned how to treat the horses on their own. It had been a time of upheaval and change, but at last life had begun to settle down again. If Daddy did contact them, then surely there would be many more changes to cope with.

Amy shut her eyes. It felt as if a distant storm cloud was looming ominously on the horizon. With a shiver, she tried to blank the thought out of her mind.

℮℈

Amy woke up early the next morning. The air was still and frosty when she took her pony, Sundance, for an early morning ride.

When she returned forty minutes later, Amy heard the familiar noisy rattle of Ty's pickup coming up the drive. She put Sundance away in his stall and strode down the yard to greet him.

"Hi," she called. "How was your Thanksgiving?"

"Pretty good," Ty called back, slamming the truck's door shut and running his hand through his dark hair. Slim but muscular, he stood only a few inches taller than Amy. "How about you? I guess it was probably kind of hard."

Amy shrugged. Having worked at Heartland for the last two and a half years, Ty knew her so well that it was pointless trying to pretend otherwise. "It wasn't easy," she admitted, "but we made it through." Not wanting to think about it anymore, she changed the subject. "I turned Daybreak and Melody out in the afternoon."

"How were they?"

As they walked up to the tack room, Amy filled him in. "Daybreak isn't having any trouble finding her independence," she said. "I think the sooner we teach her to lead the better."

Ty nodded. "We can start today."

"How about this morning?" Amy said. "I'm meeting Matt at the mall this afternoon."

Ty raised his eyebrows. "Oh, I see, you and Matt have a date, huh?"

"Come on!" Amy exclaimed. "For your information, Soraya's going to be there, too. We're *all* going Christmas shopping together." She shook her head. "Honestly! What's wrong with everyone here? Matt's just a friend — that's all!"

After the horses had been fed and the stalls cleaned out, Amy and Ty went to Melody and Daybreak's stall. Their goal was to teach Daybreak to walk to the field on a lead rope instead of letting her just run loose and follow her mother as she had the day before.

Amy knew that it was very important that Daybreak learn to be led. Her mom had always said that learning to accept the restraint of a halter and lead rope was the most important lesson you could teach a young horse. But her mother had been totally against training techniques that involved any kind of physical domination. She believed a horse should learn to submit willingly to the handler. *Force destroys trust,* she had always said, *and without trust, there can never be a true partnership.*

Amy remembered those words as she walked to Daybreak and Melody's stall. She had been handling the little filly regularly to try to gain her trust. Although at first Daybreak had resisted, Amy had been calm and persistent with her, and now she would stand while Amy ran her hands over her head, legs, and body. Admittedly, Daybreak didn't seem to enjoy it, but she accepted it and that was the main thing.

"How about I take Melody, and you follow with Daybreak on the lead?" Ty said. Amy nodded as they headed to the stall. She knew she had to be careful, that she shouldn't use the lead rope to pull or force Daybreak but simply to guide her in the right direction. If the foal stopped, then Amy would have to place her arm around the foal's hindquarters and try to encourage her to move forward with a gentle nudge. Amy had seen her mom do it many times, and she was confident that they wouldn't run into any problems.

As Ty opened the stall door, Melody whinnied a greeting. "Hi, girl," Amy said. Daybreak was standing behind her mother. Amy clicked her tongue, but the little foal gave her an arrogant look and didn't move.

"We'd better just thread the lead rope through the back of Daybreak's halter rather than hooking it to the metal ring," Ty said, starting to put on Melody's halter. "Then if something happens and she *does* get loose, the end of the rope will just slide through the leather. We don't want to risk her running around the yard with the rope attached to her halter."

Amy nodded. What Ty said made sense. As she approached Daybreak, the filly turned her hindquarters to Amy and lifted one back leg warningly. "Come here," Amy said, neatly sidestepping the filly's back end and closing in on her head. Almost before Daybreak knew what was happening, Amy had slipped the halter over her nose and was slipping the end of the rope through the back.

Daybreak tossed her head but Amy kept hold of her. "Don't be silly," she said. "It's going to be OK."

Ty led Melody out of the stall. At first, all went well. Daybreak, realizing that she was going to the field, followed her mother eagerly. Amy simply held the lead rope loosely and walked alongside her. Then, halfway up the path, Daybreak suddenly stopped.

"Walk on," Amy encouraged, clicking with her tongue. Daybreak did not move. The foal watched Ty lead her mom farther away, but she stubbornly stood still. "Walk on," Amy repeated, now putting her right hand around the filly's hindquarters and pressing lightly. Whenever she had seen her mom apply the same method, the foal had always walked forward, but not Daybreak. Throwing her head high, she dug her heels in. Amy increased the pressure. "Come on, Daybreak, walk on," she said more firmly.

But instead, Daybreak shot backward with a speed that took Amy completely by surprise. The lead rope slid through her hands, and she instinctively grasped it. As the rope tightened and halted her with a jerk, Daybreak gave an enraged squeal and rose on her back legs, her head fighting against the restraint, her front legs striking the air.

"Let go of the rope!" Ty shouted, looking around and seeing the foal rearing, pulling full force against the lead. "Let go, Amy, or she'll go over!"

But Amy had realized the danger the foal was in and had already loosened the rope. The end of it slithered through the halter, and Daybreak was free. As her front hooves landed on the path with a thud, she plunged sideways and came to a trembling halt.

"Easy, Melody, easy," Ty said, trying to calm the mare, who was struggling to get to her foal. "What happened?" he demanded.

"I don't know. I put my arm behind her and she just went crazy," Amy exclaimed, staring at the foal. Her heart was pounding as she thought about how close Daybreak had come to toppling over backward and really hurting herself. Amy stepped toward the foal to try to catch her again, but she shied away.

"Leave her," Ty said quickly. "She needs to calm down. Let's just put them out in the field."

"But if we do that, she'll think that by fighting the lead she can get her own way," Amy protested.

"I know, but look at her," Ty replied. "She's too tense

to learn anything now. She'll fight us no matter what we do."

Amy hesitated. It was a hard decision. If they gave in to Daybreak now, she would have learned a damaging lesson, but Ty was right. They didn't want to have to use force to teach her a lesson. And Daybreak was not in the mood to give in. Nodding her head, she reluctantly agreed, going ahead of Ty to open the field gate.

Ty led Melody into the field and unhooked her lead. Keeping a wary eye on Amy, Daybreak shot through the gate and up to her mother. Stopping dead, the filly shoved her head against Melody's belly and began to feed. She didn't seem at all fazed by what had just happened. In fact there was an almost mischievous wag to her tail as she suckled.

Amy felt awful. It was Daybreak's first lesson in leading, and it had ended disastrously. "What did I do wrong?" she said. "I never saw a foal act that way with Mom. Did I scare her or something?"

"Scare her?" Ty echoed in astonishment. "I don't think so. You saw her. She wasn't scared of that lead, she was fighting it."

"But why?" Amy said.

"She's just headstrong," Ty said. "You can see it in her eyes. You know, most horses are willing to give in. In the wild, the herd follows the lead stallion or mare. When we train them, most horses follow us in the same way.

But sometimes you'll get one who isn't willing to give in — a horse who would have been a lead stallion or mare in the wild. Some horses will fight anything." He looked at Daybreak. "They used to be called rogue horses."

"But Mom always said that there's no such thing!" Amy burst out. "Horses aren't born bad, it's people who make them turn bad."

"I know," Ty said quickly. "And I agree with her. But there are exceptions. Some horses are born with a strong instinct to fight control. I think Daybreak's one of them. It doesn't mean she's bad, but she won't be easy to train."

"She'll learn," Amy protested. "She's only a baby."

Ty didn't say anything for a moment. "Yeah," he said at last. "You're probably right. She's young, and if we're patient, she'll learn." He fastened the gate. "But I don't think we should try leading her in the open again for a while."

Amy nodded. He was right. Until Daybreak was willing to listen to her cues and walk on a lead, they shouldn't work with her in areas where she could get loose. She looked at the fiery little filly in the field and acknowledged that training her to be led was going to be far more difficult than she'd imagined.

❧

Lou dropped Amy off at the mall just after two o'clock. Lights glittered on every tree and storefront and

canned seasonal songs boomed out through the loud-
speakers as she made her way through the crowds. Just
about everyone seemed to be out shopping. At last she
caught sight of Matt and Soraya, waiting by their old
meeting place, Huckleberries Ice Cream Parlor.

"Hi!" she gasped as she reached them. "Sorry I'm late.
I got busy with Daybreak and turning out and —"

Matt grinned. "Yeah, yeah — why change the habit of
a lifetime?"

"I'm not *always* late," Amy protested.

"Only ninety-nine point nine percent of the time,"
Soraya teased. "So what shopping do you still have
to do?"

"Everything," Amy said as they started to make their
way through the crowds. "All my Christmas gifts — *and*
it's Ty's birthday soon. I've got to get something for
that."

"Hang on, I need to find a belt for Scott," Matt said,
dashing into a leather store they were just passing.

Soraya looked at the display of belts, wallets, and
coats in the window. "Maybe I should get something for
Ben," she said. "What do you think?"

"I don't know," Amy said. It was a tough question
to answer. She knew Soraya liked Ben, but he hadn't
shown any sign of asking her out even though they
seemed to get along very well. "I mean, you don't want
to get him a gift if he doesn't give you anything."

"I know," Soraya said. "But what if he does get me something and I don't have anything for him?"

They frowned at each other, appreciating the difficult dilemma. "I know. I'll try to find out if he's going to get something for you," Amy said.

Just then, Matt came back out of the store with a shopping bag in his hand. "That's one gift down," he said with some satisfaction. He dug a list out of the pocket of his jeans.

"You're so organized," Amy said as they set off through the crowd again. "How do you know what to get everyone?" Her own shopping was much more haphazard. She tended to buy things on impulse, not having any clear plans but just waiting until she saw something she liked.

"I just asked everyone before I came here. It makes my life a lot easier." Matt grinned as Amy began to think that she should have been a bit more practical.

"But you didn't ask me what *I* wanted," she teased.

"Me, neither," joined in Soraya.

"Er . . . well, it's a surprise," Matt started. "Now, I could go to that store that sells aromatherapy stuff," he said, consulting his piece of paper. "I want to get something for my mom. You know about aromatherapy, Amy. Can you give me some help?"

"I thought you made a list!" Soraya exclaimed.

"I did, but — er — Scott was the only one around when I filled it out," Matt admitted. "I'm guessing at the rest."

"So much for making your life easier," Amy laughed. "Come on, let's go." She began to think what *she* might buy at the aromatherapy shop — some oils for Lou, maybe something for Ty. Suddenly, her eyes fell on a group of three girls approaching from the opposite direction. "Oh, great!" Amy groaned to Soraya. "Look who it is."

Ashley Grant and her two friends, Jade Saunders and Brittany Phillips, were sauntering through the crowd, perfectly put together in their designer clothes. Ashley Grant was Amy's least favorite person in the world. Her family owned a highly successful hunter-jumper stable called Green Briar. It was close to Heartland, but the methods they used couldn't be more different. Val Grant, Ashley's mom and the head trainer at Green Briar, believed in using force and firm discipline.

"Maybe we should go to the music store first," Soraya said, grabbing Amy's arm. She wanted to avoid Ashley's crew as much as Amy did.

"Is Dan still dating Brittany?" Amy asked Matt as they followed Soraya. Dan Evans was one of Matt's friends from the soccer team.

"Yeah," Matt replied. "They've been seeing each other a lot. We all went to a movie on Wednesday night — Ashley came, too."

Amy raised her eyebrows sarcastically. "That must have been fun."

Matt smiled. "You know, she's not that bad when you get to know her."

Amy stared at him in disbelief. "This *is* Ashley Grant we're talking about, isn't it?"

"She's sent me an invitation to her Christmas party," Matt said.

This piece of information was enough to stop Soraya and Amy in their tracks. "What? *You're* going to the Grants' Christmas party?" Soraya exclaimed.

"Hey, not just me," Matt said hastily, seeing the expression on their faces. "There's a lot of guys from the soccer team going."

Amy could hardly believe it. Every year the Grant family held a huge Christmas party at their very large house. Ashley talked about it for weeks in advance and afterward; it was considered *the* party to be invited to by the people at high school who cared about that sort of thing. However, the invitations were very exclusive, and even Matt, who was very popular, had never been invited before. "And you're going to go?" Amy said incredulously.

"Sure." Matt shrugged. "Why not?"

"Amy! Wait up!"

Amy swung around. It was Ashley. She was pushing her way across the crowded mall, waving.

Amy's muscles tensed. The only time Ashley ever spoke to her was to make sarcastic comments, usually about Heartland. However, Amy knew there was no way of getting out of talking with her. Lifting her chin, she held her ground. "Hello, Ashley," she said coolly as Ashley reached her. She waited for the cutting remark, but to her surprise Ashley's lips, perfectly defined by rose-red lipstick, curved into a smile.

"Hi," she said. "How are you?"

Amy stared at her in astonishment. Ashley Grant had just asked her how she was and, even weirder, sounded like she *meant* it. She looked at Soraya and saw that her friend's brown eyes were wide with disbelief.

Hardly noticing that Amy hadn't replied, Ashley carried on. "Did you have a good Thanksgiving?" She paused for a fraction of a second. "It must have been busy with all the horses you have at the moment. Were Ty and Ben around to help?"

Having expected a standoff, Amy could hardly get her head around this new-style Ashley. Feeling like she was in some sort of crazy dream, she shook her head. "They both had the day off."

"Are they going to be away for the whole weekend?" Ashley asked.

"No, Ty's back today and Ben's back tomorrow," Amy said.

"Oh, that's good," Ashley said. She looked up at Matt with her catlike green eyes. "Did you get my invitation for the party, Matt?"

"Yeah," Matt replied. "Thanks."

Ashley turned back to Amy. "You must come as well, Amy," she gushed.

"You're inviting *me* to your party?" Amy said in absolute astonishment.

"Of course." Ashley said it as though it was the most natural thing in the world for her to invite Amy. Suddenly, she seemed to remember Soraya. "You, too, Soraya," she added. "I'll drop your invitation off with Amy's tomorrow."

Amy frowned. The last thing she wanted was to go to the Grant's party. "It's OK," she began, about to tell Ashley not to bother, but Ashley interrupted her.

"Sorry, Amy," she said, smiling widely. "I'd really love to stay and talk but I have to go. I'll see you tomorrow!" And with that she turned and flounced away to where Jade and Brittany were waiting.

For a moment, Amy and Soraya stared after her in stunned silence.

"Did I just dream that?" Soraya said in a strangled voice. "Or did Ashley really just come over here and invite us to her party?"

"It *has* to be a dream," Amy said.

"Or else there's something totally weird going on," Soraya said. "Like aliens have come and taken over Ashley's body."

"Come on, you guys," Matt protested. "I told you — Ashley's not that bad. It's Thanksgiving. She must have remembered about your mom, Amy. Maybe she was just trying to be friendly."

Amy and Soraya looked at each other. At the same moment they shook their heads. "No — aliens," they said together.

Soraya grinned at Amy. "So, are we going to go?"

"Are you kidding?" Amy asked. She caught a look of disappointment cross Soraya's face and she frowned in surprise. "Why? You don't want to, do you?"

Soraya hesitated. "Well, it could be kind of fun, but there's no way I'm going without you," she added hastily.

"Yeah, come!" Matt urged. "I'll have a way better time if you guys are there."

Amy frowned. She didn't really want to go, but Matt and Soraya both looked so eager. "Let's see if Ashley actually delivers the invitations first," she said skeptically.

❧

Much to Amy's surprise, Ashley turned up at Heartland the next morning. It wasn't ideal timing. Having decided to work with Daybreak once more before trying to use the lead rope again, Ty was holding the foal in the field while Amy was running her hands over the filly's body, legs, and head.

Daybreak had managed to stay reasonably still for five minutes. However, at exactly the moment that Val Grant's silver Mercedes pulled into the driveway, Amy decided to try to persuade Daybreak to move forward a step. The second the little filly felt Amy's left arm pressing around her hindquarters, she shot violently backward in protest. Amy jumped back just in time to avoid being trampled, and Ty barely managed to hang onto Daybreak.

"Looks like you've got a difficult one there!"

"Oh, no," Amy groaned to Ty as she looked around and saw the figure of Val Grant striding toward the gate.

Ashley followed her mom. Ashley had on expensive black breeches, and her pale blond hair fell to her shoulders in a gleaming sheet. She looked like a glamorous model from a magazine advertising riding clothes — the models whom Amy suspected had never even touched a currycomb. Still, Amy suddenly felt very aware of the straw in her own hair and the stains all over her worn jeans.

"Causing you some problems, is she?" Val Grant said, nodding at Daybreak.

Amy gritted her teeth. "Nothing we can't manage," she said. "We just need some time."

Val Grant ignored her words. "I wouldn't let a little thing like that mess with me," she said, her eyes narrowing as they swept over the defiant filly. "I'd tie one of her legs up and force her to the ground. Keep her there until she gives up fighting. You need to show her who's the boss right from the start."

A string of angry words leaped into Amy's mouth, but before she could say anything Ty stepped forward. "That's not how we go about things here," he said levelly, only the darkening of his eyes revealing how angry *he* was, too. "But thanks for your advice, Mrs. Grant."

Val Grant's face hardened, and for a moment tension crackled in the air. It was broken by Ashley producing a bundle of envelopes from her pocket. "Here are the invitations to our party," she said, handing them to Amy. She'd been so busy looking around at the yard that she had hardly seemed to notice the exchange between her mom, Amy, and Ty. "I brought one for you as well, Ty, and one for Ben. Do you think he might like to come, Amy?"

Amy was still fuming from Val Grant's comments. "Why don't you ask him yourself?" she said hastily. "He's over there."

Ashley spun around. Ben was walking across the yard with a water bucket in his hand. "Ben!" Ashley called out, waving.

Ben looked around. He had only met Ashley once before, and for a moment a frown creased his handsome face as he tried to place her. But then Amy saw a look of recognition dawn in his eyes. "Hi," he said, coming over. "It's Ashley, isn't it? You're one of Amy's friends."

Ashley flicked her long hair back and smiled up at him. "That's right," she said. "I met you at the show last weekend. This is my mom, Val. Mom, I want you to meet Ben Stillman."

"Pleased to meet you," Ben said, holding out his dirt-caked hand to Val Grant.

Val looked at Ben with interest. "You're Lisa Stillman's nephew, aren't you? From the Fairfield Arabian Stables?"

"Yeah," Ben said. "My aunt sent me to Heartland to learn about treating problem horses."

Val Grant snorted derisively. "Well, I'm not sure what she thinks you'll be learning."

Ben looked confused.

"We just stopped by to drop off some invitations for a family party we're having in two weeks," Ashley stepped in quickly. "There's one for you. I thought with you being new in the neighborhood you might like the chance to meet some people." She fluttered her long eyelashes at him. "Oh — you *will* come, won't you?"

"Sure," Ben said, looking pleased. "Thanks for asking me."

Ashley held his gaze. "It's my pleasure."

Instantly, it was like a light had come on in Amy's head. *That was it!* That was why Ashley was being so friendly — she liked Ben, but she couldn't invite him to the party without asking everyone else, too. Suddenly, it all made sense.

But what about Soraya? Amy glanced anxiously at Ben for a sign he was attracted to Ashley, but to her relief he was simply smiling in his usual easy way.

"Well, I guess I'd better get back to work," he said. He turned to Val Grant. "Nice to meet you, Mrs. Grant."

"You, too, Ben," Val replied.

"See you," Ben said to Ashley, and then with a quick smile at Amy and Ty, he headed back to the water tap.

Ashley watched him go and then turned around. "Come on, Mom, let's go. See you at school, Amy," she added almost curtly as the Grants walked back to their car.

"OK," Ty said slowly, looking down at the invitation in his hand as Ashley and Val got into the car. "Do you have any idea what *that* was all about?"

"Yep," Amy said, and explained her theory to him.

"So, Ashley likes Ben!" Ty repeated in astonishment.

"I'd bet on it," Amy replied. "That's the only reason she'd invite us to the party. Did you see the way she was looking at him?" She dropped her voice in an imitation of Ashley's husky purr. "Oh, Ben, you really *must* come."

Ty grinned. "Poor Ben — do you think he has any idea what he's in for?"

"I don't know, but I guess it's only fair to warn him,"

Amy said. She headed down to the faucet where Ben was just rinsing his hands. "Looks like you've got a fan," Amy said. Her voice was teasing, but inside, her heart was thumping. She hoped — for so many reasons — that he wasn't going to say he liked Ashley.

A look of surprise crossed Ben's face. "What do you mean?"

"Ashley Grant," Amy said. "Ben!" she exclaimed seeing his blank look. "You can't tell me you missed the way she was flirting with you."

"Ashley?" Ben said incredulously. "That girl who was here just now?"

"Yeah, blond, skinny, looks like a model," Amy said.

Ben shrugged. "She's not my type. I met a lot of girls like that when I was living at my aunt's — rich, beautiful, and almost always boring."

Amy felt a rush of relief. "So, you're not interested?" she asked casually.

Ben shook his head. "I'm not ready to get involved with anyone yet. There's enough going on in my life, with Red, and learning about things here, and trying to spend time with my mom again." He picked up the bucket. "But this party sounds like fun. Are you, me, and Ty going to all go together?"

Amy shook her head. She knew Soraya and Matt wanted her to go, but she really didn't want to. "I don't think I'm going."

"Why not?" Ben said, surprised.

Amy shrugged. "It's not really my crowd. I don't think Ty will go, either."

Ben looked disappointed. "You've got to be kidding. I only accepted the invitation because I thought you guys would go. I don't want to go by myself."

Amy felt bad. It was mean to make Ben go alone. He would hardly know anyone there. And what would Soraya say if Ben decided not to go because of Amy and Ty?

"Come on, Amy," Ben pleaded. "Don't do this to me. You've got to come."

Amy thought for a second. "All right," she said. "I'll come." As much as she hated to admit it, there was a little part of her that was curious about the Grants' house and what their famous party might be like. And who knew when she'd be invited again.

"You will?" Ben looked very relieved. "Thanks. I owe you one."

Amy returned to Ty, who was handling Daybreak's legs again. "Well, I guess I'm going to the Grants' party after all," she sighed.

"Why?" Ty said in surprise.

"Ben told Ashley he'd go, and I'd feel bad if he went alone. We're the only people he knows around here," Amy explained. She looked at him. "You should come with us, Ty."

Ty shrugged. "I don't know Amy. It's not really my

kind of thing . . ." he hesitated. "But if you and Ben are going, then it might be fun." He stroked Daybreak. "She's pretty calm now. Should we try again?"

Amy nodded and positioned herself at the side of the foal. "You're sure you don't want to try Val Grant's suggestion?" she teased.

Ty's eyes met hers. "Quite sure," he said, and they both smiled.

The training session with Daybreak didn't go well. Time after time, when they applied gentle pressure to her hindquarters to encourage her to move forward, the little filly either ran backward or simply refused to move. Amy and Ty grew warmer and warmer from the workout and soon took off their heavy winter jackets.

"We can't give in," Amy said through gritted teeth after fifteen minutes. "She *is* going to move forward."

Even Ty, whose patience was normally endless, was beginning to look exhausted. "Come on, girl," he encouraged, taking a deep breath and taking hold of the halter again.

Suddenly, Daybreak took a tiny step forward.

"Good girl!" Amy cried, immediately releasing the pressure she had been applying under the foal's tail.

"It's about time," Ty exclaimed.

Amy rewarded Daybreak by rubbing her head. Most

horses love being stroked, but the little foal looked at Amy mutinously — not pulling away from the caress but not looking as if she was enjoying it, either. Amy sighed. It would be nice if, just once, Daybreak showed some affection.

"Let's call it quits for the day," Ty said, wiping his arm across his forehead.

As they released the foal, Daybreak shook her head, wheeled around, and plunged away, every muscle in her body declaring independence now that she was free. Amy watched as she cantered around the field. She loved the fire that burned so strongly within Daybreak. The challenge would be to harness that fire and channel it so that Daybreak wanted to work with, rather than against, them. Picking up her jacket, Amy left Ty to shut the gate and walked toward the front paddock deep in thought.

"Amy!"

Amy looked up. Lou was getting out of her car, a bundle of mail from the mailbox at the end of the driveway in her hand. Her eyes were bright as she waved a pale-blue envelope at Amy.

"Amy! Hurry up! It's a letter from Daddy! Come and see what it says!"

Chapter Three

Amy stopped dead in her tracks, her eyes locked on Lou. Having put the other mail on the roof of the car, Lou was tearing open the airmail letter, her face flushed with excitement. Amy felt her stomach suddenly tighten. *A letter from their father.* She walked slowly toward her sister.

Lou's eager blue eyes were scanning the page. "He says he's really sorry he didn't get to see us. And he wants to come and visit."

Amy peered at the unfamiliar handwriting. It was slightly slanted, the letters neat and precise.

"Oh," Lou said suddenly. "He says he wants to meet in February. He'll be over here on business then."

For one brief second, Amy found her mind catching

on the word "business." *Business — what sort of business? What does he do?* And then she registered the flatness in Lou's voice. "February?" she echoed. "That's three months away."

Lou nodded, and Amy saw that the excited glow in her sister's eyes had been replaced by a faded look of disappointment. "I guess he must be busy until then." She looked at the letter again. "There isn't even a telephone number, so I can't call him to see if he can come sooner. There's just an address." She handed the letter to Amy.

Tim Fleming, Amy read on the back, *Oak Farm, Willoughby, Gloucestershire, England.* She turned the letter over and skimmed the contents.

My dear Lou,

Thank you so much for your letter. I so wanted to meet you and Amy when I came over, but your grandfather told me to stay away. I can't blame him for that — I know he was only trying to protect you. I just wish you could know how much I've wanted to see you, how often I've thought about you — my two girls. What are you like now? Who do you take after? I would dearly love to meet up with you both. Unfortunately, I can't return to the States at the moment, but perhaps in February? I'll be in New York on business then so I could fly down and visit. I'm sorry it can't be sooner but things are a bit difficult right now —

*I'll explain when I see you. Till then, take care, give my love
to Amy, and remember that I think about you both every
day.*

    All my love,
      Daddy

Amy had to struggle to compose her thoughts. *Give my
love to Amy.* She reread the words three times. It was as if
an invisible thread were stretching across the world,
linking her with the father she had never really known.
But she didn't want his love. What right did he have to
suggest that she did? He wrote as if he had just been
away on vacation, not missing from her life for twelve
long years. And there wasn't even a single mention of
their mom.

She handed the letter back to Lou. "What are you going to do?"

"I don't know," Lou replied slowly.

"It's not that long till February," Amy said.

Lou stared down at the letter and didn't reply.

&

For the rest of the day, Amy tried not to think about
the letter. She didn't want to think about meeting
Daddy. She wanted to block the whole thing from her
mind. That evening, she called Soraya and told her all

about Ashley's visit. "You should have seen the way she was flirting with Ben!"

"Oh, great," Soraya groaned. "Like I stand a chance if Ashley's after him."

"But he's not interested in her," Amy told her. "I asked him." She wondered whether to tell Soraya Ben's comment about not wanting to get involved with anyone at the moment, but she held back. There was no point in depressing Soraya, and besides, she reasoned, he might not have really meant it. She tried to remember what he'd said about Ashley. "Ben said he'd met tons of girls like her before, and that they were all boring."

"Oh, come on!" Soraya exclaimed. "If Ashley's boring, then what am I?"

"Interesting," Amy said.

"Interesting!" Soraya exclaimed. "That makes me sound like a total freak."

Amy grinned. "Stop worrying. You are *not* a freak! So, are you going to come over here to get ready for the party? Ben said he'd give me and Ty a lift. I'm sure he can squeeze all of us in."

"Then definitely," Soraya said. "There's no way I'm showing up at Ashley's on my own."

"Soraya! It's only a Christmas party," Amy said.

"Correction: the Grants' Christmas party," Soraya

said dramatically. She changed the subject. "So what else did you do today besides hanging out with Ashley?"

"Well, Lou got a letter from our dad," Amy said. "He wants to come and see us in February."

"February!" Soraya replied. Amy could hear the surprise in her friend's voice. "But that's months away."

"I don't care," Amy said, her voice getting harder.

"Really?" Soraya said.

"Yes, really," Amy replied. "He can do what he wants as far as I'm concerned. It's Lou who wants to see him, not me."

Later that evening, Amy thought about what she'd said. It was true. She didn't care what her father did. But at the back of her mind, there was a haunting suspicion — was it that she didn't care or that she didn't *want* to care? There was a huge amount of difference.

Heartland's stalls were all full, so the next two weeks raced by as Amy juggled her time between the horses, school, and seeing her friends. But as usual, every spare minute she had was spent working with Ty and Ben in the barns. She was also trying to avoid being alone with Lou in case the conversation turned to Daddy. However, to her relief, Lou made no attempt to bring up the subject when they were alone, and when they were with Jack neither of them spoke about it, in case it would upset him. Grandpa wasn't looking well — the cold he had picked up the night of Daybreak's birth seemed to be lingering and the cough was getting worse. Amy and Lou tried to persuade him to see a doctor, but he kept putting it off.

With everything that was happening, Amy managed to push the letter to the back of her mind. Whenever thoughts of it crept back to disturb her, she forced herself to think about Daybreak instead. Despite Amy and Ty being patient and gentle, the little filly was still resisting their attempts to train her. Some days she would move forward when Amy gave her the cue, but mostly she would simply refuse to acknowledge her and would fight them every step of the way. Amy was starting to get worried. With each day that passed, Daybreak was getting physically stronger and harder to manage.

"I just don't understand why she's being like this," she said to Ty on a Friday afternoon as they looked over Daybreak and Melody's stall door after yet another unsatisfactory training session with the foal. "We've done everything we should."

"I was looking at one of your mom's books this morning," Ty said. "Maybe we should have handled her more in the first twenty-four hours after she was born."

Amy thought back to Daybreak's first day. "But we

were letting her bond with her mother," she said, remembering how they had decided to leave handling the little foal until the following day for that reason.

"I know," Ty said. "But this book said that if you handle a foal first thing, it will bond with you as much as with its mother. They call it 'imprinting.' But you have to do it that first day. After that it's too late."

"But I spent that first night in Melody's stall." Amy frowned. "And Mom never had a problem with the foals she handled, and they weren't even born here, they were close to two or three months old when she started working with them."

"But I bet none of them was as headstrong as Daybreak," Ty said. "I'm not saying we can't train her. I just think we'd have better luck if we'd been more hands-on from the start."

Amy looked at the little filly. She was lying down in the straw, her muzzle resting on one of her slender front legs, her hind legs curled up beneath her. Her dark eyes were focused on them — fearless, intelligent, and confident. Amy turned to Ty. "So what do we do?"

"I guess we've just got to be patient," Ty replied. "But we should try using some oils to calm her, so she'll listen better. Vetiver oil's relaxing. It's good for bold, headstrong horses."

Amy nodded. At Heartland they often used aroma-

therapy, herbs, and Bach Flower Remedies to help deal
with horse's behavioral or emotional problems. "I'll get
some vetiver from the tack room," she said.

"OK," Ty said. "I'm going to groom Jasmine and
Dancer."

Amy walked across the frosty yard to the tack room
where the essential oils were kept in the medicine cabinet. Taking out the vetiver and jojoba oils and an empty
bottle, she put thirty milliliters of the jojoba into the
empty bottle and then added twelve drops of the vetiver.
It was very important to dilute potent oils like vetiver
into a base oil to prevent them from irritating the horse's
skin. She was closing the cabinet when Ben came into
the tack room with a grooming kit.

"Hey, what are you doing?" he asked, looking at the
solution in the bottle with interest.

Amy was eager to get back to Daybreak and quickly
replied, "Just working on something for Daybreak."

She was about to leave the tack room when she
caught sight of Ben's disappointed face. Amy felt a pang
of guilt — Ben was working at Heartland so he could
learn about the alternative therapies they used. She and
Ty were so used to working together that they often forgot to explain the treatments to him.

"She's being real stubborn. Do you want to come and
see what I'm going to do?" she asked him.

"Sure," Ben said. He dumped the grooming bucket in the trunk and joined her.

As they walked by the old stable, Amy saw a ladder leaning against the eaves. Grandpa was standing near the top, replacing some missing shingles on the roof. All of a sudden, his upper body folded over in an intense coughing spasm.

Amy stopped at the foot of the ladder. "Are you OK, Grandpa?" she asked when his breathing returned to normal.

Wiping his mouth with his sleeve, Jack looked down and attempted a smile. "I'm just fine," he said, his blue eyes watering. But suddenly, he started to cough again, his hand grasping at his chest as if he were in pain.

Amy felt concerned. "You don't sound fine at all," she said forcefully. "You have to see the doctor. At least you should get off the roof until you're feeling better. If you're not careful, you could fall off."

"I've got to finish this before the weather gets really bad," Jack said, determinedly picking up another shingle. "Then I'll go in and call the doctor."

"All right, but you have to promise me you will," Amy sighed. Knowing how obstinate Grandpa was about these kinds of things, Amy reluctantly gave up.

"He's been up there all afternoon," Ben told her as they walked out of Jack's earshot.

They reached the warmth of the barn. Amy unbolted the stall door. Daybreak was still lying down. She lifted her head and stared at Amy with wary eyes. "First we've got to see her reaction to the prepared oil," Amy explained to Ben. "If she likes it, I'll massage a little into her muzzle."

"If she likes it?" Ben echoed. "What do you mean?"

"Watch," Amy said. As she headed toward the little foal, Daybreak scrambled to her feet. "Steady," Amy soothed, quickly grabbing the little foal's mane before she could swing her haunches around. Grabbing the filly's nose with her free hand so that she had some control of the foal, she unscrewed the top of the oil bottle and offered it to Daybreak to smell. At first she threw her head back in defiance at being held, but then the fragrant scent of the oil reached her nostrils. Blowing out in surprise, she seemed to forget about fighting Amy and lowered her muzzle close to the bottle. Amy held the bottle tightly in case Daybreak suddenly decided to nibble it out of curiosity. The filly sniffed the oil with each nostril and then, lifting her head, she rolled her top lip back and showed her teeth.

"She likes it," Amy said, pleased.

"How do you know?" Ben asked.

"If she didn't, she'd just have sniffed it once or she'd have turned away and put her ears back," Amy said.

"You can't treat a horse with something they instinctively don't like. Somehow they seem to know which oils will help them and which won't. You have to listen to the horse and trust her to guide you."

"So what do you do now?" Ben asked curiously as Daybreak lowered her head to sniff the oil again.

Amy poured a little of the diluted oil into the palm of one hand and then handed Ben the bottle to hold. "Now I massage her with it," she said, catching hold of Daybreak's nose again and beginning to work the oil into the skin just between the filly's ears. "It might not work immediately, but hopefully there should be a gradual change in her over the next few days. If nothing happens after a week or two, then we'll have to try something else." Turning her attention to Daybreak, she focused on massaging in the oil. For once, the foal stood calmly, her delicate nostrils trembling as she breathed in and out. Enjoying this unfamiliar moment of peace between them, Amy began to feel a flicker of hope — maybe the oil would be the solution to Daybreak's problems.

"There," Amy said at last, when the oil was completely massaged in. "I'll do that twice a day for a week. If she isn't any easier to work with after that, then we'll try something different."

As they left the stall, Ben looked puzzled. "But how does it actually work?" he said.

"Well, no one knows for sure," Amy said. "But it's thought that as the chemicals in the oil are inhaled and absorbed through the skin into the bloodstream, they reach the emotional center of the brain where they affect the horse's mood and attitude." She saw the slightly skeptical look in Ben's eyes. "Mom always said as long as it works, it doesn't matter how it happens." She bolted the stall door and took the bottle from Ben. "Come on, let's start on the hay nets."

Amy woke early the next morning. As soon as she got dressed she went to see Melody and her foal. Melody whinnied when she saw her and came over to nuzzle at Amy's hands. Amy rubbed her head and looked at Daybreak. The foal was standing in the back of the stall. Amy held out a hand. "Hi, girl."

With a squeal, Daybreak swung around and gave a discreet buck, her tiny ears flat against her head. Amy sighed. It didn't look like the vetiver oil was working just yet.

After she had fed the horses, she went back down to the house to grab some coffee. To her surprise, the table was set and Lou was bustling around the kitchen, cooking breakfast. "I've made some waffles," she said brightly as Amy came in. "Sit down. There's maple syrup and bacon on the table and some fresh coffee in the pot."

Amy stopped and stared. "You made *waffles*?" she said. Normally, the only person in the house who cooked breakfast was Grandpa. If Lou was in charge of breakfast, it was never anything more than a bowl of cereal and a slice of toast.

"Yes, I thought I'd cook for us all," Lou said. "I told Grandpa to sleep in for a while. I heard him coughing really badly last night."

"Again?" Amy looked worried. "I told him he had to get an appointment at the doctor's."

"Yeah, and he has," Lou said. "But the doctor can't see him for three days." She busied herself around the kitchen. "Now, sit down. Are waffles OK? Or do you want some scrambled eggs? I can whisk some up in no time."

"OK," Amy said, realizing there was something on Lou's mind other than breakfast. "What's going on, Lou?"

"What do you mean?" Lou said. "I just thought it might be nice if I organized breakfast for a change."

Amy raised her eyebrows. "But all *this*?" She pointed at the table piled with waffles, bacon, orange juice, and steaming coffee.

Lou hesitated and then suddenly her shoulders sagged. "Well — you're right," she admitted, sinking down onto a chair. "There *is* a reason." She looked at the tablecloth. "I've — I've got something to tell you."

From the tone of her sister's voice, Amy could tell that she wasn't going to like what she had to say. "What is it, Lou?"

Taking a deep breath, Lou lifted her eyes. "I've made a decision, Amy," she said resolutely. "I'm going to England. I have to find Daddy."

Chapter Four

Amy stared at her sister, her heart thudding. "What do you mean?"

"I've booked a flight to London on Wednesday." Lou's eyes begged her to understand. "I know Daddy said he's coming over in February, but I can't wait till then. Thanksgiving made me realize that life's too short for family rifts. I need to see him now."

"But it's only two weeks till Christmas," Amy stammered, hardly able to take in what Lou was saying. "How long will you be gone?"

"I'll be back before then," Lou said. "I've got his address, so it won't take me long to find him."

"But can't you just call him?" Amy said desperately. "There has to be some way you can find his phone number and talk to him that way. Why do you have to go to see him?"

"I tried to get the number, but the operator said it wasn't listed," Lou replied. "Anyway, I don't just want to talk to him. I want to *see* him and get this all sorted out." She grasped the back of a chair. "I've been waiting twelve years for this, Amy. Please say you understand."

For a moment Amy battled with a desperate urge to beg Lou not to go. Part of her was terrified that she would never come back. *Don't go, please don't go,* she thought.

"Amy?" Lou said.

As much as Amy wanted her to stay, she knew she couldn't convince her. This was something Lou had to do. She took a deep breath. "I understand," she whispered, the words hurting her as she uttered them.

But she was rewarded by the look of intense relief that crossed Lou's face. She hugged Amy. "Thank you. It means a lot to me. I know it's hard at the moment with Grandpa not being very well and —"

"I'm fine. What do you mean I'm not well?"

Amy and Lou turned around. Jack was standing in the kitchen doorway, pale and tired.

"Grandpa," Lou stammered. "How long have you been there?"

"I just came down." A frown deepened on Jack's face as he looked from one granddaughter to the other. "What's going on?"

Lou glanced nervously at Amy. "I think you'd better sit down, Grandpa."

Lou told him what she'd just told Amy. "I have to go, Grandpa," she said.

Amy looked anxiously at their grandpa's face. She knew how he felt about their father. How would he take the news?

For a moment, Jack didn't say anything, but then he squared his shoulders. "Lou," he said quietly, "I've always said that you should follow your heart, and if that's what it's telling you to do, then that's what you should do." He looked at Amy. "We'll get along fine, won't we, Amy?"

"I'm not going to leave you completely on your own," Lou said quickly. "I've called my friend Marnie — you remember her, Grandpa? She came to visit that time you were away at Glen and Silvia's. Well, she's got some time off and said she'd love to come and stay again. I'll leave instructions so she can take over my work while I'm gone. She'd already talked about coming to visit over the holidays — her parents are away in Fiji for Christmas and New Year's, so it works out perfectly. When I asked her if she'd come a little early, she was really excited."

Amy was surprised but pleased. She liked Lou's friend Marnie a lot.

"What about Scott?" Grandpa asked. "Have you told him?"

"No, not yet. I just made up my mind yesterday that I was going to go, and I wanted to tell you two first," Lou replied. "He's stopping by this morning. I'll tell him then."

Amy remembered something. "But you'll miss his reunion dinner."

"He'll understand," Lou said confidently. She smiled, looking as if a weight had lifted from her shoulders now that she had told them. "I just can't wait to see Daddy again. Imagine his face when I just show up at his door."

"Lou, you've got to remember you don't know anything about your father's life now," Grandpa said warningly. "Maybe you should write to him and let him know you're coming."

"There's no point," Lou said. "I'm flying out on Wednesday, so I'll probably arrive before a letter could get to him anyway." She saw the concern on Grandpa's face. "Daddy wants to see me — his last letter made that clear."

"Yes, I know, but —" Grandpa broke off as Lou's face narrowed. "Look, just be careful, honey," he sighed, "that's all I'm saying."

Lou smiled. "I will." She hugged him. "You worry too much, Grandpa. Everything will be fine, you'll see."

❧

After breakfast, Amy went out to the barns. Going up to Daybreak and Melody's stall, she leaned over the door, thinking about Lou's trip.

"Hey, you." Amy turned around to see Ty coming down the aisle toward her. He frowned as he saw her face. "What's up?"

"It's Lou," Amy sighed. "She's going away." Miserably, Amy told Ty about Lou's plans. "What if she doesn't come back?" she said.

"She'll be back," Ty said reassuringly. "Her life's here now. You know she decided that when she gave up her job in New York."

"But what about Daddy? What if he wants her to stay with him?" Amy voiced her worst fears.

"Hey." Ty squeezed her shoulder. "Take it easy, Amy. A lot has changed since she last saw him. Lou has changed."

Amy took a deep breath and forced herself to stay calm.

"Come on," he said practically. "You can't stand around worrying about it. Let's get started on the stalls."

❧

At eleven o'clock, Scott drove up and parked outside the house. "Hi!" he called, jumping out as Amy came down the path with a wheelbarrow. "Is Lou around?"

"She's in the house," Amy replied, for once hoping that he wouldn't come and talk to her.

He took a white envelope out of his pocket. "The tickets for the dinner arrived. Do you know if Lou has gotten her dress yet?"

Just then, the front door opened and Lou came out. "Hi, Scott," she said quietly.

Scott bounded over to her. "Hi," he said, seeming not to notice her subdued manner. He kissed her enthusiastically. "Our tickets are here."

Lou glanced in Amy's direction.

Amy immediately took the hint. "I better go and turn Jasmine and Sundance out," she said, hastily dumping the wheelbarrow.

As she headed back to the barn, she heard Lou say, "Scott — we need to talk."

Out of earshot, Amy stopped and took a deep breath. She couldn't help wondering how Scott would take the news about Lou going away.

Ten minutes later, she heard his engine start up. She headed cautiously toward her sister.

Lou was watching Scott drive away. Her face looked worried.

"How did it go?" Amy asked her tentatively.

Lou sighed and turned round. "It was all right —
although he was disappointed about the dinner," she
said. "I don't think he understands why I have to go to
England right now." Lou paused for a moment. When
she next spoke, her voice had a note of doubt in it for the
first time. "I — I am doing the right thing, aren't I,
Amy?"

Amy struggled hard against her feelings. She knew
Lou needed her support. "Of course you are," she said
as convincingly as she could. "You heard what Grandpa said this morning. You've got to follow your heart,
Lou."

Lou looked slightly happier. "Yes," she said. "You're
right. That's what I'm going to do."

🙢

Soraya came around that afternoon, and as soon as
the horses were fed, she and Amy went inside to get
ready for the Grants' party. Amy had been saved the
trouble of worrying about what to wear by the simple
fact that she only had one dress that was suitable. It was
a pale, shimmery, silver color with tiny straps and se-
quins and beads sewn along the hem of the floaty skirt
that ended just above her knees. Lou had bought it for her
at Bloomingdale's a year ago, when Amy and Grandpa
had gone to visit her in Manhattan. Amy had worn it

that night in the city, but since then it had stayed in the back of her closet.

"I love that dress," Soraya said as Amy took it out of its garment bag. "You should wear it more often."

Amy grinned. "Yeah, it would be perfect for mucking out the stalls." She shook out the dress. "What are you going to wear?"

Soraya took down two outfits from the back of Amy's door — a long black dress with a low back and a short lilac shift dress with tiny butterflies embroidered on the bodice. "I couldn't decide. Which do you think?"

Amy looked from one to the other. "The lilac," she said decisively.

"But you haven't even thought about it," Soraya complained.

"I just like it best," Amy said. She couldn't see the point of agonizing about clothes for hours.

"But which do you think *Ben* would like?" Soraya asked.

"Both of them," Amy grinned, going over to her desk and putting a CD on. "Now, stop worrying and take a shower."

🙠

An hour later they were just about ready. Amy sprayed on some perfume borrowed from Lou while Soraya finished fixing the clips in her hair. Amy's party dress swished elegantly as she walked, and her strappy silver shoes emphasized her slender ankles and calves. Usually when Amy went out she just wore a dash of mascara, but tonight Soraya had persuaded her to be more adventurous. She had used silver eye shadow and eyeliner to emphasize her gray eyes, and she had even blow-dried her long silky hair.

"You look great!" Soraya said as Amy looked critically at her reflection in the mirror.

"I just feel weird," Amy complained. "It doesn't look like me."

"You could always put your riding boots on underneath your dress," Soraya said teasingly.

"Don't tempt me!" Amy smiled.

Soraya put the final clip in place.

"I love your hair like that," Amy told her.

Soraya anxiously worked a few curls down around her face.

Amy glanced at her bedside clock and saw that it was nearly seven o'clock. "Come on, we'd better go downstairs!"

Grandpa and Lou were sitting in the kitchen watching a game show. Grandpa was drinking a steaming hot mug of honey and lemon tea. They looked up as Amy and Soraya entered.

"Wow! You should take a shower more often!" Lou teased.

Feeling very self-conscious despite her sister's sarcasm, Amy hurried across the kitchen and grabbed her jacket.

"That's a gorgeous dress, Soraya," Lou said.

"Thanks," Soraya smiled.

"You both look perfectly beautiful," Jack said warmly, getting to his feet. As he did so, his chest rumbled with a single deep cough.

Amy looked at him in concern. "You sound awful, Grandpa."

"I'm all right," Grandpa said. "And if it doesn't get any better, I've got that doctor's appointment."

"All right, Grandpa," Lou said. "But promise you'll stay inside tomorrow."

"I'll see," Jack replied.

Just then there was the sound of a truck drawing up outside the house. Grandpa looked out the window as a horn blew. "It looks like your ride is here. You girls enjoy yourselves."

"Yeah, have fun!" Lou said.

"We will," Amy replied. "See you later."

Ben and Ty were standing by the pickup. Ben gave an appreciative whistle as he saw them. "Hey, look at the two of you!"

"You like?" Soraya said, giving a twirl.

"I do," Ben grinned.

Amy found her eyes drawn to Ty to see his reaction.

"You look really nice," Ty said to her.

Amy felt the blood rush to her cheeks. She hurried to the door of the pickup, glad that the darkness hid her blush. "It's freezing out here," she said quickly to disguise her embarrassment.

Ben held out his hand to Soraya with a fake English accent. "May I escort you to your carriage, ma'am?"

Soraya giggled. "You may," she said, pretending to curtsy. Taking his hand, she let him help her into the pickup. Amy and Ty followed her in.

It was a squeeze with all of them squished in the bench seat. Sitting between Ty and Soraya, Amy was acutely aware of Ty's legs pressed against hers. Trying to reposition herself, she leaned back and then flinched slightly as their shoulders touched.

"Here," he said, moving over to make more room for her.

"Thanks," Amy muttered, not wanting to look him in the eye. The air was cold but her cheeks were burning. She looked down at her lap. She couldn't imagine why she felt the way she did.

❧

The Grants lived in a sprawling mansion on the edge of town. A wide gravel driveway led to the grand front entrance, which was decorated with an oversize holly wreath. On either side of the door were tall Christmas trees, covered with thousands of twinkling fairy lights.

Candles flickered in every window. "Whoa!" Soraya said. "It looks like a palace out of some fairy tale."

"It looks like an electrical fire hazard to me," Amy muttered, but even as she spoke she had to admit that she was impressed. The place looked beautiful.

As they entered the house, the smell of balsam and pine seemed unusually strong. There were Christmas trees in every room, and the mantels were weighed down with swathes of dark green foliage and shiny red berries. Waiters bustled around with trays of drinks and beautifully prepared morsels of food — miniature quiches, smoked salmon canapés, delicate asparagus spears, tiny pizzas, and Thai prawns. For the first time, Amy began to see why everyone made such a big deal about the Grants' Christmas party. She looked around at the masses of people. "I wonder if Matt's here yet?"

"Over there!" said Soraya, nodding to a group standing by one of the Christmas trees. Matt was talking with Dan and Ashley, Jade and Brittany.

"Matt!" Amy called out as she waved.

Matt looked around. His handsome face broke into a smile. "Hey, Amy," he said, coming over. "You look great."

"As do you," she replied.

"Well, hi there!"

Amy glanced over Matt's shoulder. Ashley had left her little group and was heading through the crowd toward them. She was wearing a stunning silvery-green long dress that shimmered in the lights. Noticing how her blond hair cascaded over her shoulders in a riot of artfully styled curls and her green eyes were emphasized by glittery mascara, Amy couldn't help but think that Ashley looked like a mermaid.

"Hi, Ashley," Amy said. Reminding herself that this was the Grants' party, she was determined to be polite. "You look lovely."

"Thank you." Ashley's eyes swept over Amy's outfit. "That's a nice dress — I remember it from the sales rack at the end of last season, but some styles don't really date, do they?" She smiled sweetly and turned to Ben and Ty. "Let me get you a drink."

Amy looked at Soraya and rolled her eyes. She knew Ashley had been trying to insult her, but it didn't faze Amy; she didn't care whether her dress was the latest look or not.

Ashley waved a waiter over and then looked up at Ben through her long lashes. "I'm so happy *you* could come," she said.

"Thanks," Ben replied, smiling easily.

"You *must* come and meet my friends," Ashley said, putting a hand through his arm. "They're *dying* to meet you."

Shooting a rather helpless look at Amy, Ty, and Soraya, Ben allowed himself to be led away.

Ty grinned at Amy. "Well, I guess we won't be seeing much of Ben this evening."

Amy glanced at Soraya. The sparkle in her eyes had immediately gone flat. "Don't worry. We'll rescue him in a bit," Amy said quickly. "We won't let her monopolize him all night."

Just then, the live band started playing in the far room. "Come on," Amy said, desperate to get Soraya to cheer up. "Let's go dance!"

🙰

At first Amy danced with Ty, Soraya, and Matt as a group, but gradually Matt started to draw her away from the other two. "You really do look amazing tonight," he said.

Amy grinned at him. "Thanks."

For a few minutes they danced without saying anything else, but Amy became conscious of Matt's eyes never leaving her face. She found herself purposely avoiding his eyes. As the song ended, the music changed tempo and slowed down.

Amy glanced around. "Well, I guess we should find Ty and Soraya," she said quickly. But before she could move, Matt had grabbed her hands.

"Don't go, I love this song," he said, the tone of his voice becoming serious.

Amy swallowed. This wasn't what she wanted at all. "But it's a slow song," she said.

"I know," Matt said, smiling at her. He slipped his left hand around her back and tried to draw her closer. "Come on, Amy. You know that I like you."

Amy pulled back. Her heart was pounding now, but she didn't want to make a scene. "Matt, I like you, too," she stammered, desperately wishing she was some- where — *anywhere* — else. "But I don't think I'm ready for anything more. If we started dating it would change everything."

"Yeah — it would be great," Matt said. He gripped her hand. "We'd be good together, Amy."

Amy saw the hope on his face. She didn't want to hurt him, but she didn't want him to go on thinking there could be something between them. It wouldn't be fair. She just didn't like him that way. "Look, Matt, I really like you as a friend. . . ."

Matt's face stiffened, and before she had a chance to go on to explain, he dropped her hand.

Amy saw the hurt in his eyes. "Matt —" she began.

Ignoring her, he turned around and started to walk away.

At that moment Soraya came bounding across the dance floor. "Ty and I are going to get something to eat," she said brightly, stopping in front of Matt. "Are you two coming?"

For a fraction of a second, Amy thought Matt was going to brush past her, but then he shrugged. "Sure."

Breathing out a trembling sigh of relief, Amy watched him walk over to join Ty at the edge of the dance floor.

"You OK?" Soraya asked her in a low voice. "That looked kind of uncomfortable."

"It was," Amy said, with feeling. "Thanks."

They followed Ty and Matt to the side of the dance floor where a long table had been set up with drinks and finger food. As they reached it, Ty looked at Amy. She was sure he must have noticed what was going on, too, but he didn't say anything. Matt's face was hidden as he leaned over the food table and filled a plate.

"Where's Ben?" Amy said.

"Where do you think?" Soraya sighed, nodding toward Ashley's group of friends.

Amy looked over. Ben was standing near Ashley's crowd. She was trying to persuade him to dance.

"Come on, you haven't danced all night," Amy heard her say.

Ben looked awkward. "Maybe later."

"Can't Ashley take no for an answer?" Amy said to Soraya.

Ashley flicked back her hair. "But this is a great song. Come dance with me." She took Ben's hand.

Ben gently freed himself. "No, thanks."

"Why not?" Ashley pouted. "Don't you like me?"

An embarrassed look crossed Ben's face. "Ashley, you've picked the wrong guy," he said. "I'm not looking for a relationship right now."

Ashley stared at him and then drew back as if she'd been slapped. "What makes you think I want a relationship!" she exclaimed, her face flushing hotly. "I only asked you to dance!"

Ben stood there helplessly as Ashley stormed off, her friends close behind her.

"Well, Ben told her," Amy said to Soraya with a giggle.

"Oh, yeah — that's real funny, Amy!" Amy swung around. Matt was standing a few paces behind her, glaring at her. "You know, Ashley might actually be upset. What if she really likes Ben?" He didn't give her time to let her answer. "You never thought of that, did you?"

Amy felt awful. She hadn't thought anyone had been close enough to hear. "Matt —" she began, not knowing what to say. She realized how insensitive her comment must have seemed to him, so soon after what he had said on the dance floor.

"Forget it, Amy," Matt said coldly as he walked off. "Just forget it."

Chapter Five

Amy looked at Soraya and Ty's stunned faces. "I'll go after him," she said quickly.

She set off across the dance floor. She felt awful. She had to figure out how to apologize to Matt. But she stopped when she turned around the corner. Matt was walking up to Ashley. At first Ashley didn't look at Matt but continued talking with Jade and Brittany. When Ashley finally turned to him, her face was hard. But then he held out his hand, and to Amy's astonishment, a look of gratitude crossed Ashley's face. With a faint smile, she took Matt's hand and allowed him to lead her onto the dance floor.

Soraya came up behind her. "What's going on?" she asked, looking bewildered. Her eyes widened as she saw

Matt and Ashley together on the dance floor. "What's Matt doing?" she gasped.

"Dancing," Amy snapped, a sharp pang of betrayal shooting through her as Matt's arms encircled Ashley's slender waist. He was supposed to be *her* friend.

"But he's dancing with *Ashley!*" Soraya said as they watched Ashley's arms curve around Matt's neck. She turned to Amy. "What happened?" she demanded. "Why did he get so mad at you?"

"I don't know," Amy lied. She saw the disbelief in Soraya's eyes. "OK, I guess he might have been a little upset because I didn't want to slow dance with him," she admitted reluctantly.

"So he asked Ashley?" Soraya said, as if she still couldn't believe it. "But he doesn't even *like* Ashley."

"Well, he certainly doesn't seem to be giving that impression at the moment," Amy said sarcastically as she saw Matt draw Ashley closer.

As she spoke, the song came to an end and the music became faster again. Amy watched Matt and Ashley, expecting to see them go their separate ways. But they didn't. Matt said something to Ashley. She smiled, and then they separated slightly. Still holding hands, they started to dance again.

Amy was still watching Matt and Ashley when she realized that Ty was standing beside her. Soraya was nowhere to be seen.

"Do you want to dance?" he asked.

Amy looked at him in surprise. "With you?"

Ty grinned. "No — with the giant nutcracker in the corner."

Amy saw the teasing glint in his eyes and smiled. "OK," she said.

They found a space on the dance floor. Trying to forget about Matt dancing with Ashley, Amy let the music swell through her mind. As her body swayed in time with the beat, she glanced at Ty. His gaze was fixed on her face. As she looked into his familiar eyes, Amy's heart somersaulted, and she suddenly seemed to lose the ability to breathe. For a moment they just stared at each other, and then without saying a word, Ty stepped closer and took her hand.

The rest of the world seemed to swirl and fade away. Amy could think about nothing except the heat of Ty's fingers clasped around hers. They moved together in time with the music, their eyes fixed on each other's face.

Amy didn't know how long they'd been dancing when Ben came up to them.

"We've got some drinks and a table to sit at!" Ben shouted over the music. "Soraya's guarding it!"

Ty dropped Amy's hand.

"What?" Amy stammered to Ben. She suddenly became aware of the crowd of people around them, the sound of talking and laughing, of Ty standing there and looking at her with an unreadable expression in his eyes.

Ben bellowed out his message again.

Amy glanced at Ty and saw his face smooth into its usual friendly expression. "Great," he said easily. "You coming, Amy?"

Amy forced herself to nod. "Sure." Her voice came out high and breathless, but Ben and Ty didn't seem to notice. Taking a deep breath to calm her pounding heart, Amy followed Ben and Ty over to the table.

It was two o'clock in the morning when they finally got back to Heartland. Ty jumped out of the pickup to let Amy out.

"Thanks for the ride, Ben," Amy said.

"No problem," Ben replied. "See you later."

Amy looked at Soraya. She was scooting over in the seat, taking advantage of the extra room now that Ty and Amy were out. But Amy thought Soraya had looked pretty happy when she was squished in next to Ben.

"Call me," Amy said, giving her a meaningful look. As far as she knew, nothing had happened between Ben and Soraya, but they had been together all evening and Amy wanted to know the details. Besides, Amy also wanted to know what Soraya thought about Matt and Ashley, who hadn't left each other's sides all night.

A grin twitched at Soraya's lips. "I will," she promised.

Amy got out. The frosty air stung her bare legs, and her breath froze like smoke as it left her lips. "Night," she said to Ty, who was standing by the pickup door. Since the moment on the dance floor they hadn't been alone together, but now she found herself looking into his eyes and felt a blush creep up her neck.

"Good night, Amy," Ty said softly.

Amy hesitated. She felt as if they were both waiting for something, but she didn't know what.

"See you later," she said breathlessly as she hurried indoors.

✷

As she got into bed and turned off the light, Amy's thoughts raced back to the moment when she'd been dancing with Ty. Shutting her eyes, she could see his face as clearly as if he were there, could feel his fingers touching hers, could feel her heart pounding. She'd never felt like that before.

But this is Ty you're thinking about, she quickly reminded herself.

She curled her knees up to her chest. It was just so confusing. How could she feel like that about Ty, of all people? *I see him every day,* she thought. *He's one of my best friends.* But still, the memory of him holding her hand came back to her. She tried to push it away. After all, she didn't even know how Ty felt. It wasn't like he'd tried to kiss her or anything.

But what if he had? she thought.

She stopped herself before she went any further. Nothing was going to happen between her and Ty — nothing!

℣

Four and a half hours later, Amy woke up to the blare of her alarm clock. She groaned and staggered out of bed. She was in the middle of mixing the feeds when Ty arrived.

"You look as good as I feel," he said, coming into the feed room.

Amy jumped at the sound of his voice. "Morning," she said, hastily trying to cover her confusion. After the events of the night before, she sort of felt that he should look different, but he looked exactly the same as he always did every morning. "I can't believe I've only had four hours' sleep," she said.

"Me, neither," Ty said. "But," his voice softened suddenly as his eyes met hers, "it was worth it."

Feeling suddenly flustered, Amy grabbed a pile of the feeds. "I'll go get started on the back barn," she said.

For the rest of that morning, she avoided being alone with Ty. Trying not to think about the night before, she threw herself into the regular routine of cleaning the stalls and taking the horses out to the paddocks. Just before lunch, she was on her way to bring Moochie and Jake in when she heard the telephone ringing. A few seconds later, Lou opened the back door. "Amy! It's Soraya on the phone!"

Amy hurried to the kitchen. Kicking her boots off, she took the phone from Lou. "Hey," she said, carrying the phone up the stairs to her bedroom and shutting the door. "How are you?"

"Fine," Soraya said, and Amy could hear the grin in her voice. "Oh, Amy, I've got a lot to tell you."

"About you and Ben?" Amy said eagerly.

"Yes!" Soraya said. "Do you remember when you and Ty were dancing?"

Did she remember? Amy didn't think she'd ever forget. "Yes," she said.

"Well, did you notice how long Ben and I were gone when we disappeared to get drinks? " Soraya asked.

Not wanting to admit that she hadn't noticed at all, Amy quickly lied. "Yes, of course. So what happened?"

"Well —" Soraya stopped.

"Go on," Amy urged.

"Well, there was a long line for drinks, so we went outside onto the veranda for a while," Soraya sighed dreamily. "It was, like, really romantic. There were loads of stars in the sky and just me and Ben standing there."

"And?" Amy said in an agony of impatience. "What happened?"

"Well, nothing happened exactly," Soraya admitted. "We just stayed there and talked. He told me all about what it was like growing up on his aunt's farm instead of with his parents and about how he feels about getting to know his mom all over again. I felt like he was being very honest. He said he could really talk to me."

"Soraya, that's great," said Amy, even though she detected some hesitation in her friend's voice. She was eager to get to the important point.

"Yeah," Soraya admitted. "I wish he would have kissed me. It would have been so perfect, but he said that he's got so much stuff going on with his mom and everything else that he just doesn't want to date anyone yet. But I don't care. I'll wait. I'll just be his friend for now, if that's what he wants." Amy could hear the happiness in Soraya's voice. "When he dropped me off at home he said he'd really enjoyed the evening and that maybe we could go out sometime."

"On a date?" Amy exclaimed.

"Well, not a date exactly," Soraya said. "But you never know — it could lead to that."

"That's wonderful!" Amy said. "Just think how mad Ashley will be if you start dating him!"

"Speaking of Ashley, what do you think's going on with her and Matt?" Soraya said eagerly.

"I think they both just wanted someone to hang out with last night, but I don't think it's going anywhere," Amy said. "He can't possibly *like* her."

Soraya suddenly sounded more serious. "But what if they do start going out? Do you think we'll have to hang out with her?"

"They won't start dating," Amy said. "Matt's got better taste than that."

Soraya didn't say anything.

"He does!" Amy insisted, trying to suppress a vision of what it would be like if Matt and Ashley were going out and always hanging on each other at school.

"Well, I guess we'll see tomorrow," Soraya said.

After Soraya hung up, Amy sat in her room, thinking about what Soraya had said. There was no way Matt and Ashley would start dating — was there?

She looked at the phone and then punched in Matt's number.

"Hello, Mrs. Trewin," Amy said when Matt's mom answered. "It's Amy. Is Matt there?"

"I think you're in luck," Mrs. Trewin said. "I just heard him get up. Let me call him for you." Amy heard Mrs. Trewin shouting for Matt and then she came back on the phone. "It must have been some party last night," she said with a laugh. "He hasn't been out of his room all morning."

"It was," Amy said.

Just then, Matt took the phone from his mom.

"Hi," Amy said brightly.

"Hello." Matt's voice sounded guarded.

Amy suddenly felt awkward. "Last night was a lot of fun, wasn't it?" she said.

"I had a good time," Matt replied briefly.

There was a pause. Amy wanted to ask about Ashley, but Matt sounded so cool and reserved that she didn't dare. For the first time since they had become friends she found herself searching for something to say to him. "So — what are you doing today?" she said at last.

"Just stuff," Matt said noncommitally. He didn't expand, and there was another uncomfortable pause.

"OK, then, I better get going," Amy said. "I — I just thought I'd call to say hi."

"Yeah," Matt said. "See you tomorrow at school."

As Amy put the phone down she realized that her face was flushed. Matt had sounded like he didn't want to talk to her at all. She remembered how hurt he had looked when she had been laughing with Soraya after Ben refused to dance with Ashley. More than anything she wished that she could take that moment back. Matt was her friend, and although she didn't want to go out with him, she had never meant to upset him. He acted as if she and Soraya had been laughing at him.

It'll be OK tomorrow, she told herself, trying to be positive. *He'll have forgotten about it by then.*

✖

But the next day she couldn't help feeling nervous when they reached Matt's stop. Matt's tall figure got onto the bus, and to Amy's relief he made his way to the seat in front of her and Soraya, just like he usually did.

"Hi," he said. He sounded normal, but Amy noticed how his eyes slipped quickly away from hers as he greeted them.

"Hey," Soraya grinned, unaware of the slight tension in the air. Amy had been too embarrassed to tell Soraya about the phone conversation she'd had with Matt. "So, what was going on with you and Ashley on Saturday night?" Soraya teased.

Matt looked uncomfortable. "We were just dancing."

"Are you going to start dating?" Soraya said. "Go on — tell us."

Amy saw how awkward Matt was looking. "Of course Matt's not going to start dating Ashley," she said quickly, wanting to stop Soraya's teasing.

But it was the wrong thing to say. Matt turned to her. "What do you mean I'm not?" he demanded.

"Well, I mean, it's *Ashley*," Amy said, taken aback by the anger in his eyes.

Matt glared at her, obviously misinterpreting her words. "It may be hard for you to believe, Amy, but there are some people who would go out with me."

Amy stared at him. "I didn't mean it that way, I just —"

Matt got to his feet. "You know, sometimes you can be so selfish. You only see what you want to see," he said, and with that he marched off to sit farther down the bus.

Amy and Soraya looked at each other in stunned silence for a moment and then Amy jumped to her feet. "Matt," she said, following him, "I didn't mean that she wouldn't want to go out with you. I meant it the other way around."

Suddenly, Matt looked very weary. "Look, just forget it," he said. "I don't want to talk about it." Opening his bag, he took out a paperback and began to read.

Glancing around, Amy was suddenly aware of the curious looks they were getting from the other students. She hesitated, hoping Matt would look up, but his head stayed resolutely bent over his book. With her cheeks burning, she made her way back up the bus aisle.

At school that day, Matt hardly said a word to Amy. He hung around with Ashley and her friends. Every so often Ashley would link her arm through his and look triumphantly over in Amy's direction.

"I don't know why she's looking at me that way," Amy muttered to Soraya at lunchtime. "Everyone's going to think that I had wanted to go out with Matt and she stole him from me."

"Sure you're not jealous?" Soraya said.

"*Jealous!*" Amy exclaimed. "Of course I'm not jealous. Matt can do whatever he wants!"

But despite her words, she had to admit that she would miss being with Matt. Not in a romantic way, like Soraya meant, but they'd been friends since sixth grade and it felt strange to see him hanging around with other people — especially Ashley and her friends.

By the time Amy got home that afternoon, she was in a very bad mood. She dumped her backpack in the empty kitchen and went upstairs to get changed. Lou was in her bedroom, packing for her trip. "Had a good day?" she asked as Amy went past.

"No," Amy replied abruptly.

"Oh," Lou said. She came to her door. "Do you want to talk about it?" she said.

"No," Amy said again, and going into her bedroom, she pointedly shut the door.

She went to the window. The cold gray sky seemed to press down on the muddy fields. Sundance and Jasmine were grazing in the field by the back barn. Amy suddenly frowned. Grandpa was working on the paddock gate. As he bent to pick up some nails, she saw him start to cough. He leaned weakly against the fence, his shoulders shaking.

"Oh, Grandpa," Amy muttered, exasperated.

She pulled off the sweater she'd worn to school and grabbed a sweatshirt, determined to go straight out and tell him to come inside. But just then she saw Grandpa stagger. He grasped at the fence, and then suddenly his knees seemed to sag. He sank to the ground with his hands clutching his chest.

"Lou!" Amy screamed, throwing her sweatshirt down and running to the door. "Lou! Come quick!"

Chapter Six

"Dial 911!" Lou shouted as she ran down the stairs and out of the house. "Call an ambulance!"

Her heart pounding, Amy grabbed the portable phone in the kitchen. It only took a few seconds to get through to the emergency medical services. "I need an ambulance!" Amy gasped when an operator answered. All the time, she never took her eyes from Grandpa's bent-over body.

By now Lou had reached him. Amy saw Lou's arms go around his shoulders, saw her turn and yell for Ty and Ben.

"Name, please," a voice spoke in Amy's ear.

"Fleming — Amy Fleming," she burst out.

"Address?"

Amy rattled off the address.

"And what seems to be the problem, Amy?" the woman on the other end of the phone asked calmly.

"It's my grandpa," Amy said, barely able to get the words out. "He's collapsed."

She was asked more questions — what exactly had happened, whether Grandpa was conscious, how old she was, who was with her. She answered them almost without thinking as she watched Lou, Ty, and Ben help Grandpa to his feet. Half carrying him, they brought him back to the house.

"An ambulance is on its way," the woman said. "I need to know as much as you can tell me about your grandpa's condition so I can help you to help him while you wait for the ambulance to arrive. Does he have a fever?"

"I don't know," Amy replied anxiously. "Hang on —"

Lou came through the door, opening it wide so Ty and Ben could help Grandpa inside. "Lou! They want to know about Grandpa's condition. Does he have a fever?" Amy gasped.

"Here, I'll talk to them." Lou grabbed the phone from her. "Lou Fleming here," she said.

Amy looked at Grandpa. He was conscious but his lips were blue and he was breathing in quick, shallow gasps. Beads of sweat stood out on his forehead.

As Amy watched Ty and Ben lower Grandpa onto the sofa, she heard Lou answering the woman's questions. Despite her obvious concern, Lou's voice was brisk and in control. "I see," she said, scribbling notes on the pad. "Keep him warm, change his clothes if they're damp, give him fluids if he'll take them. And how long did you say the ambulance would be?"

Amy crouched beside Grandpa's side. "It's going to be OK. The ambulance will be here soon."

"No ambulance. I'll be all right," Grandpa said, wheezing between each sentence. His normally sharp blue eyes looked dazed and confused. "Got to fix the gate."

"The gate!" Amy exclaimed. "The gate doesn't matter, Grandpa!"

A spasm of coughs burst from Jack, his face screwing up in pain.

Amy couldn't bear it. "What's the matter with him?" she cried, looking at Ty and Ben.

"Pneumonia." There was a click from behind them as Lou replaced the hand set. They all turned to look at her. "That's what the woman thinks from his symptoms." She hurried to Grandpa's side. "Come on, we've got to keep you warm and dry until the ambulance arrives."

The next few hours passed in a blur for Amy. The ambulance seemed to take forever to get there. However, when it did, the paramedics immediately assessed the situation. Grandpa was lifted into the ambulance and given an oxygen mask. Then the doors shut and the ambulance set off for the hospital. Leaving Ben and Ty to take care of the horses, Amy and Lou followed in Lou's car. Neither of them spoke much on the way. Staring out the window, Amy just kept seeing Grandpa collapsing on the ground, his face contorting in pain.

At the hospital, Grandpa was taken away immediately, and she and Lou had nothing to do but wait. At last a young female doctor came to find them to confirm that Jack did indeed have pneumonia.

"So what exactly does that mean?" Lou demanded.

"Well, as you may know, pneumonia is a serious inflammation of the lungs," Dr. Jane Marshall explained. "The air sacs in the lungs fill with liquid, and this keeps the correct amount of oxygen from reaching the blood." She paused, watching them to see if they were following. "Your grandfather has a bacterial form of pneumonia. It can affect people of all ages. It's most likely to take hold in someone whose immune system has been weakened in some way by an illness. When a person's resistance is lowered, the bacteria that normally live in the throat can work their way into the lungs. That bacteria causes the air sacs to become inflamed."

Amy thought about the cold that Grandpa had picked up when helping Melody to foal. "Grandpa has had a bad cold for several weeks," she interrupted. "He hasn't rested and it's just gotten worse and worse."

"That would certainly weaken his immune system," Dr. Marshall replied, nodding.

"How long will it take him to get better?" Lou said quickly.

"It all depends on how he responds to treatment," Dr. Marshall said. "The inflammation is very severe, which is why he has such a high temperature and is in such pain. We're giving him antibiotics to combat the infection and painkillers to help ease the pain in his chest from coughing. He's also on a respirator, which will help get his oxygen levels back to normal. Providing he responds to the treatment and there are no complications, we're probably looking at a hospital stay of about a week."

"Can we see him?" Lou asked.

"Yes, but just briefly," Dr. Marshall said. "We're still trying to stabilize his condition."

Amy and Lou followed her down a succession of long white corridors. At last the doctor stopped outside a door. "He's in here," she said.

Amy took a quick look through the glass in the door. Grandpa was lying in bed on his back, his eyes closed. Long thin tubes traveled from machines into his arm and nose.

Dr. Marshall opened the door. "You can go in," she said quietly.

They walked into the room. Lou sat down by the bed and took Grandpa's hand. "Hello, Grandpa," she murmured.

Amy followed her. Standing beside Lou's chair, she saw Grandpa's eyelids blink. "Lou?" he whispered hoarsely, turning to look at her.

Lou squeezed his hand. "Yes, Grandpa, I'm here. So's Amy."

Grandpa's clouded blue eyes found Amy. She felt a lump of tears form in her throat as she saw the confusion in his face. "Hello, Grandpa," she said, longing to hug him but not quite daring to because she didn't want to interfere with the tubes.

"Where am I?" Grandpa asked.

"In the hospital," Lou replied. "You've got pneumonia, and you need to stay here a while — until you get better."

Amy half expected Grandpa to object, but his illness seemed to have drained all the fight from him. He nodded wordlessly.

Lou squeezed his hand. "We're going home now. You need to rest." She leaned forward and kissed his cheek. "But we'll come back tomorrow. You take care now."

She stood up and let Amy take her place. "Bye, Grandpa," Amy whispered. "We love you."

A faint smile caught at the corners of Grandpa's mouth. "I love you both, too."

🙦

Amy and Lou got back to Heartland at ten o'clock that night. They found the lights on and Ben and Ty waiting for them.

"How's Jack?" Ty asked as soon as they got out of the car.

"They're still trying to stabilize him, but they think he's going to be OK," Lou said. She explained about the pneumonia, her voice as brisk as the doctor's. "We can go back first thing in the morning."

"Well, don't worry about the horses," Ben said. "We'll take care of them, won't we, Ty?"

Ty nodded.

"Thanks," Lou said gratefully. "That would be a real help."

"Do you want us to do anything now?" Ty asked, looking from her to Amy.

"No, we'll be fine," Lou said. "You two go home."

Ben said good night and went over to his pickup, but Ty paused by Amy. "How are you doing?"

She shrugged. She had a feeling that if she spoke she would start to cry.

Ty squeezed her shoulder. "Look, I'll see you tomorrow," he said, and walked to his truck.

As she watched his taillights disappear down the drive, Amy felt tears spill down her cheeks.

"Hey, Amy," Lou said, noticing and hugging her. "Don't cry. You heard what the doctor said. Grandpa's going to be OK."

Amy wiped her sleeve across her eyes. "But it was just seeing him like that, Lou — with all those tubes, barely able to breathe."

"I know," Lou said. "But he'll be out in a week or two." She took Amy's hands. "Come on, we need to be strong — for Grandpa."

☘

Amy stayed home from school the next day. She and Lou went to the hospital in the morning. They found Grandpa looking a bit brighter. He was still pale, but his skin had lost the horrible blue-white tone of the day before. An IV was still attached to his arm, but the tube had been taken out of his nose.

Lou sat down next to him and Amy sat on the edge of the bed. "How are you feeling?" Lou asked him.

"Better," Grandpa said weakly.

"That's good," Lou told him. "Now, you're going to do exactly what the doctor says, aren't you? You're going to rest and get better."

Jack nodded. "I've learned my lesson." He looked at Amy. "How's everything with the horses?"

"Fine," she reassured him. "Ty and Ben said they'd cover for you."

"You don't need to worry about a thing," Lou said quickly. "I'm going to cancel my trip to England. We'll easily manage till you come back."

Jack stared at her. "No, Lou — you can't cancel it, not for me."

"Don't be silly, Grandpa," Lou said. "I'm not going away while you're in the hospital."

"But I don't want you to stay because of me." Grandpa pulled himself up so he was leaning against his pillows. "No, I mean it, Lou," he insisted as Lou opened her mouth to argue. "I want you to go." The exertion of sitting up made him start to cough. He bent over, his face turning white as he grasped at his chest.

Amy looked at Lou in alarm. Lou quickly picked up a glass of water from beside the bed. "Here, Grandpa, drink this."

Grandpa swallowed a few sips. "Please," he said weakly as he caught his breath and his coughs died away. "Go to England like you'd decided."

Lou shook her head. "I couldn't. Now let's stop arguing about this."

"Go," Grandpa said, starting to look agitated again. "I won't be happy till I know you're going, Lou."

Lou hesitated. She looked at Amy, who shrugged.

"OK, Grandpa — I'll go, as long as the doctor says you're getting better," Lou said slowly.

Amy stared at her sister.

"Good," Grandpa whispered, a look of relief crossing his face as he sank back against the pillows. His chest moved up and down in short, shallow breaths.

"You're worn out," Lou said, looking worried. "We'd better leave."

But Jack shook his head. "No. I want to tell you something first."

"We'll come back later, Grandpa," Amy said, standing up. "You can tell us then."

"I want to tell you now," Grandpa insisted. "It's about your parents."

Amy sat back down on the bed slowly, wondering what he was going to tell them.

Jack took a wheezing breath. "It's something your mother never told you. I realized this morning that if anything ever happened to me you might never know. Or if you found out, you might be upset that you heard it from someone else."

"What are you talking about, Grandpa?" Lou asked.

Grandpa paused for a moment. "There's no easy way to say this," he said, looking from one sister to the other, "but your parents got a divorce three years ago."

Amy stared at him. "A divorce! What do you mean?"

She saw the shock on Lou's face. "Mom would have told us!"

"She didn't tell anyone apart from me," Jack said. "Your father initiated the divorce. Your mom didn't want to agree — despite everything, she still loved him — but as you know, she'd already turned down his attempts to reconcile and try to get back together. I think she probably felt she had no choice."

Amy struggled to take it all in. She'd always thought her mom and dad had stayed married. *Well, does it really matter?* she thought. *It's not like they were ever going to get back together.* But it mattered to her, and she couldn't pretend it didn't. Being divorced seemed so much more final than just being separated. "Why didn't you tell us before, Grandpa?" she asked, trying to understand.

Jack sighed. "I wanted to respect your mother's wishes," he said. "She didn't tell you when she was alive, so I didn't see how I could after she died. I don't know why she decided not to tell you, and I feel like I've betrayed her. But I couldn't keep it from you — you have the right to know."

There was silence for a moment and then Lou spoke. "Thank you for telling us," she said, squeezing Grandpa's hand. "You did the right thing."

Jack looked at her anxiously. "I hope it won't stop you going to England."

Lou shook her head. "Divorced or not, he's still my daddy." She smiled. "The only thing that will stop me going is if you don't start getting better."

Looking as if a weight had been taken off his shoulders, Jack leaned back against the pillows. "Oh, I'll get better," he said, smiling weakly back at her. "I'll be out of here in no time — just you wait and see."

Chapter Seven

"So, how is he?" Ty said. He and Ben were waiting for Amy and Lou when they pulled into Heartland's driveway.

"It looks like Grandpa will be in the hospital for at least a week," Lou explained, stepping out of her car. "But then, providing there are no complications, he can come home and recuperate here."

"That's great news," Ben said, looking relieved.

Lou smiled. "Yes, it is."

Not a single muscle in Lou's face betrayed the impact of Grandpa's recent announcement. Amy wasn't so able to hide her feelings. "I'm going to get changed," she said, just wanting to be on her own.

In her bedroom, she sank down on her unmade bed. Mom and Dad were divorced. She thought about the letter her father had written to her mother, begging for a reconciliation. *I'll never stop loving you,* he had written in that letter. She picked up the photograph of her mom and Pegasus that she kept beside her bed.

As always when she saw that photograph she'd have given anything to have her mom back for half an hour — to talk to her again, to tell her how much she loved her. But this time she would ask her mom questions. Why did she keep Daddy's letter secret? And why hadn't she told them about the divorce?

❧

When Amy finally went back downstairs, she found Lou, Ty, and Ben in the kitchen having coffee.

"Do you want some?" Lou asked, gesturing toward the coffeepot.

Amy shook her head. She didn't feel like talking. "I'll go get started on the grooming."

Ty jumped to his feet. "I'll go with you," he said, dumping his coffee mug in the sink and following her outside.

"Are you all right?" he asked as they walked up the path.

Amy nodded. She didn't want to talk to anyone, not even Ty.

Ty looked up at the sky where dark rain clouds were gathering on the horizon. "We should hold off on the grooming," he suggested, "and take Daybreak for a walk before that rain sets in."

"OK," Amy agreed, feeling relieved. She knew that if she was with Daybreak she wouldn't have a chance to think about anything else. And right now, that was just what she wanted.

They headed toward the back barn. As always, before trying to lead Daybreak out, Amy spent at least five minutes running her hands over the filly's body and legs, trying to get her used to being handled.

Daybreak seemed quieter than normal. "She's being good," Amy said to Ty, who was holding the filly's head. "Maybe the vetiver oil's working."

"Or maybe she's not feeling very well," Ty said, pointing to Daybreak's muzzle. "She might have a cold."

Amy joined Ty and saw that Daybreak had a runny nose. She felt worried. She knew that any illness in a young foal had to be watched carefully. Foals less than eight weeks old are especially vulnerable because they don't have an older horse's ability to fight off disease. "I'll check her temperature," she said.

Amy went to get the thermometer. "One hundred degrees," she said, checking the reading twice to make sure. "So it's normal."

"Well, I guess we don't need to call Scott then," Ty said. "But we should keep an eye on her for the next few days."

❧

Later that morning, Amy saw Scott's Jeep coming up the driveway. "Amy!" he said, looking worried as he got out of the car. "Ty called me this morning and told me about Jack. I came as soon as I could. How is he?"

"He's a bit better," Amy said. "The hospital said that he'd probably be out in a week." She was about to ask him to take a look at Daybreak when the back door opened and Lou came out.

"Scott, what are you doing here?" she said, surprised.

"Ty told me the news," Scott said, going over to her. "I came as soon as I could." He held out his arms. Lou stepped forward and Scott's arms folded around her. Bending his head, he kissed her hair. "I'm really sorry."

It was such an intimate moment that Amy felt awkward witnessing it. She started to back away.

Scott noticed Amy's expression and broke away from Lou. "It must have been terrible for both of you," he said, including Amy in his glance. "So what exactly did the hospital say?"

Lou explained. "I don't know how we're going to make him take it easy when he comes out." She looked at Amy. "You can't let him do anything outside while I'm away — no fixing the roof or gates."

"I won't," Amy said. She saw Scott frown.

"What do you mean — when you're away?"

Lou's cheeks flushed pink. "I'm — I'm flying to London tomorrow."

Scott stared at her in astonishment. "What? When Jack's in the hospital?"

"Grandpa wants me to go," Lou said quickly. "He knows how important this is to me. I feel like there's something missing from my life. I get this empty feeling whenever I think of Daddy."

Amy saw Scott's jaw tighten. "I see," he said flatly. "I didn't realize how hard it's been on you."

"I want to stay — really, I do," Lou went on, "but Grandpa won't hear of it — he's made me promise to go."

"*Made* you?" Scott snapped angrily. "Jack would never make you do anything, Lou. You know that. This is your choice. Don't try to pretend it's not."

Lou looked astonished at his outburst. "Scott —"

"No, Lou," Scott interrupted icily. "If you want to go chasing halfway around the world after the father who deserted you when your grandpa is right here sick in the hospital, then that's fine — it's your decision. Just don't try to justify it to me." Scott's face was thunderous as he strode down to his Jeep and, slamming the door shut, drove away.

Amy looked quickly at Lou. She was staring at Scott's car with a shocked expression on her face and then, tears suddenly filling her eyes, she rushed into the house.

Amy followed her.

"Lou?" she said tentatively, going over to her sister, who was standing by the kitchen table.

"I can't believe Scott said those things!" Lou exclaimed. She sank down in a chair. "Of course, I don't want to leave Grandpa while he's sick, but he understands. You heard him today — he wants me to go."

Well, maybe he wouldn't if he thought that you really wanted to stay, Amy thought to herself, but looking at the confusion on Lou's face she bit back her words.

"If I could be in two places at once, I would be," Lou said, shaking her head. "But I have to go to England. You know that."

Amy didn't know what to say. It would be really tough to deal with everything on her own, but she knew it would be selfish to ask Lou to stay.

Lou stared at her. "You agree with Scott, don't you?" she said. "You think I should stay."

"I don't," Amy lied quickly, not wanting to upset Lou even more. "You *should* go to England, Lou. Grandpa will get better soon, and it'll only make him feel guilty if you stay." Her words sounded false even to her own ears, but Lou didn't seem to notice. She nodded, looking slightly comforted.

"You're right. I mean, it's not like I'm going to be gone long." She managed a smile. "Thanks, Amy. It's good to know I've got your support."

Amy smiled, trying to ignore the voice in her head that said, *Just tell her that you think she should stay.*

Lou sighed. "I wish Scott could be so understanding." A frown crossed her face. "I can't believe he blew up at me like that."

"He was probably just hurt," Amy said. She saw her sister's surprised expression. "I mean, you did say that you have an empty feeling. That can't have made him feel too great."

Lou looked at her in astonishment. "But I didn't mean that my life was bad, just that it sort of feels incomplete without Daddy."

"But that's not what it sounded like," Amy said.

"Scott *knows* how important he is to me," Lou said. "He won't take it that way." She shook her head and stood up. "You'll see. He'll think it over and change his mind."

❦

Amy got up at six o'clock the next morning to see Lou off. "Now, you've got Marnie's phone number," Lou checked as she put her bags in the car.

Amy nodded. "What time do you think she'll arrive?"

"Around five o'clock," Lou said.

"What about you?" Amy said. "Where can I contact you?"

"I'll call from London when I get in," Lou said. "I'll be

staying one night in a hotel near the airport, then I'll head to Gloucestershire, where Daddy lives." She gave Amy a slightly nervous look. "I'm not sure where I'll be staying after that."

Amy hugged her. "Good luck."

"Thanks," Lou said, hugging her back. "Now remember to go back to school tomorrow."

"I will," Amy sighed. They'd agreed that she would stay home from school until Marnie arrived. "But I don't see the point of going back at all. Term ends soon anyhow, and I don't have any more tests."

Lou smiled at her. "You should still go back until then."

They embraced for a long moment and then Lou got in the car and drove off. Amy waved until her sister's car disappeared from sight, then she looked around. It was still dark, and suddenly everywhere seemed very quiet. She went into the house, trying to get used to the strange sensation of being on her own.

Back in the kitchen the silence pressed down on her. She switched the radio on and sat down at the table, wondering what to do. Picking up the latest issue of the local paper, she tried to read, but the words just wouldn't sink in. So much had happened in the last few days — the Grants' party, Grandpa going into the hospital, and now Lou leaving. She shook her head. The Grants' party seemed like weeks ago.

At last she gave up trying to read, and pulling on her jacket and boots, she went outside to get started on the horses.

When Ben arrived, he volunteered to finish off the jobs that Grandpa had been working on. Amy agreed, thinking that at least then Grandpa wouldn't be tempted to go outside when he came home from the hospital. But it meant that she and Ty had to do all the stalls and exercising on their own. The phone — which Lou normally answered — seemed to ring constantly with inquiries from prospective clients and people looking for horses to rehome. As Amy answered the sixth call that morning, she silently thanked Lou for getting the portable phone. How had they managed before?

Walking into the feed room after the last call, Amy remembered that she needed to call the feed merchants because they were running low. That was when she began to realize, for the first time, just how much Heartland's day-to-day business depended on her sister.

At lunchtime, Ty drove Amy to the hospital.

"Did Lou get off all right?" Grandpa asked them as they sat down.

"Yes, she left at six this morning," Amy answered.

Grandpa nodded. "And how's everything going?"

"We're getting along just fine," Amy told him. "Ben's

been fixing the fences this morning and just about all the horses are done," she lied, trying not to think about the five stalls that still needed to be mucked out, the unswept yard, and the fact that it looked like none of the horses were going to get worked that day.

Grandpa looked relieved. "Good," he said.

Amy looked at him with concern. He was paler than the day before, and when he coughed, she saw his knuckles clench the bedsheets. "How are you feeling?" she asked.

It seemed to take an effort, but Grandpa managed to smile. "I'm on the mend," he said. "Don't you worry about me. You've got enough to think about with the horses and all."

But Amy wasn't convinced he was improving, and as they left she told Ty that she wanted to find a doctor. They asked at the reception desk and were told to wait. They had been sitting on hard plastic chairs in the lobby for fifteen minutes when, to Amy's relief, Dr. Marshall came to find them.

"I'm afraid your suspicions are correct. Your grandfather's not responding as well as we had hoped to the medication," she admitted to Amy. She saw Amy's face became pale. "But please be assured, we're monitoring his progress carefully."

Amy's throat felt dry. "Will — will he still be able to

come home soon?" she asked, trying to sound calm. "Before Christmas?"

Dr. Marshall looked at her sympathetically. "I'm afraid I can't say at the moment. We'll just have to see how he feels over the next few days."

Amy nodded, unable to speak.

"Do you have any other questions?" the doctor asked.

Ty looked at Amy, who shook her head. "Thank you," he said to the doctor.

Amy followed him out of the hospital, her stomach churning with worry.

"He'll be all right, Amy," Ty said, looking at her white face as they went outside.

Desperately wanting to believe him, Amy nodded.

"If it was anything more serious the doctor would have told you," Ty reassured her.

Amy took comfort from his words. "Yeah," she whispered, trying to be positive. But she couldn't help thinking that Grandpa was sicker than she'd even imagined.

Chapter Eight

Just as they were finishing feeding the horses that evening, a yellow sports car came up the drive. "Marnie!" Amy exclaimed as it stopped in front of the house and a tall, slim woman in her twenties got out. Dumping the hay nets she was carrying on the ground, Amy raced toward the driveway.

"Hi, Amy!" Marnie said, hugging her. Marnie's blond hair bounced on her shoulders as she looked around. "Wow!" she said. "It's so good to be back."

Amy grinned, feeling really happy for the first time in days. She knew Marnie loved Heartland — that was one of the reasons why she liked her so much. "I love your car," she said, looking at the shiny new sports car.

"Well, there have to be some perks to working in the city," Marnie said. She took a deep breath of the frosty air. "Though I have to admit that being here again really makes me wonder."

"Do you want some help with your stuff?" Amy offered.

Marnie glanced at the hay nets lying on the ground. "No, you go ahead and finish what you were doing. I can manage — am I in the same room as last time?"

Amy nodded. It was her mom's old room. "Just make yourself at home," she said.

Marnie smiled at her. "That'll be easy. This place feels like home already."

After unpacking and walking through the barns, saying hi to all the horses and to Ben and Ty, Marnie declared she would make supper. "I'll go shopping tomorrow," she said, peering into the almost empty fridge. "But for tonight, I could make us some pasta with —" She looked in the cupboards. "Tuna, tomato, and olive sauce. How does that sound?"

"Great," Amy said.

"Do Ty and Ben want to stay for supper?" Marnie asked. "I can easily make enough to feed all of us."

Amy went to ask. "They both said they'd love to," she said, returning to find that Marnie was already preparing enough for four hungry people. "They're just finishing up in the feed room," she smiled.

Marnie handed her a jar of olives. "Then let's get this food moving. You start chopping those tomatoes, and I'll put the pasta on."

Amy sat down at the table and got to work. A few minutes later, Ben and Ty came in. They shrugged off their jackets, washed their hands, and began to help. The kitchen, which only that morning had seemed so silent and empty, was now suddenly bustling with life.

In the middle of the supper preparations, the phone rang. It was Lou.

"Lou!" Amy exclaimed. "Hi! Where are you?" Hearing her exclamation, Marnie, Ty, and Ben immediately quieted down.

"I'm in London," Lou replied. "At the hotel."

"How was the flight?" Amy asked.

"We were a bit late getting in, but it was OK," Lou said. "How's Grandpa?"

Amy hesitated. She didn't want to worry Lou now that she was so far away. "Fine," she said.

"That's good." Lou sounded very relieved. "I haven't been able to stop thinking about him, wondering if I made the right choice."

"Marnie's here," Amy said quickly, wanting to get off the subject of Grandpa. "Do you want to say hello?"

"Yeah!" Lou replied.

Amy held the phone out to Marnie, who handed Ben the cheese to grate while she spoke to her best friend.

"How are you doing?" she said, taking the phone from Amy.

Lou and Marnie spoke for a few minutes and then Marnie handed the receiver back to Amy.

"I'd better go," Lou said. "This call's going to cost me the earth. Give Grandpa a big hug for me."

"I will," Amy promised.

"And wish me luck for tomorrow," Lou said, sounding nervous. "I've rented a car, and I'm going to drive over to Gloucestershire to Daddy's house in the morning."

Amy's heart flipped. With everything that had been happening, she had pushed the thought that Lou might be seeing their father the next day to the back of her mind. "Good luck," she said.

"I'll call tomorrow night and tell you all about it," Lou said. "Bye for now."

"Yeah, bye," Amy said, and with a click Lou was gone.

"Lou sounds good," Marnie said to her as she replaced the handset on the charger.

Amy nodded slowly. "Yeah." She chewed on a fingernail. "She's going to try to find our father tomorrow."

Marnie looked at her quizzically. Amy thought she was going to say something, but she didn't. Instead she swung back into action. "OK, supper's almost ready," she said, taking the cheese grater from Ben. "Someone get the drinks together. Then we can all sit down and eat."

❧

After supper, Marnie and Amy went to the hospital. Grandpa was lying in bed, looking pale and tired. Talking seemed to hurt him and he didn't say much, but he was evidently pleased to see Marnie.

"I didn't realize he was quite so ill," Marnie said as they walked back to the car. "Lou seemed to think he was getting better when she called me last night."

"He was," Amy said. "But now I'm not so sure. Ty and I spoke to a doctor this morning, and she said he's not responding to his medication."

"You didn't mention it to Lou when she rang this evening?" Marnie said.

"No," Amy admitted, wondering whether Marnie would think she'd done the right thing. "I didn't want to worry her."

"That was probably smart," Marnie said reassuringly. "After all, she can't do anything about it while she's in England." She frowned. "Still, if he gets much worse, you should probably tell her."

Hoping that it wouldn't come to that, Amy nodded. "Yeah, I will."

❧

Amy didn't sleep well that night. One minute she was thinking about Grandpa in the hospital and the next she was thinking about Lou. In just a few hours' time Lou was going to drive up to their father's house and knock on his door. What would happen?

By the morning, Amy's stomach was knotted with tension. "Maybe I won't go to school today," she said to Marnie as they got breakfast together. "If I don't go, I could visit Grandpa this morning."

"Why don't you call the hospital and see how he is?" Marnie suggested. "He might be feeling better."

Amy agreed. But when she got through to the ward, they told her that they couldn't put her through. "I'm sorry, but he's asleep," the nurse told her. "He's had a difficult night and he needs to rest."

"Can I come see him?" Amy asked quickly.

"It might be best if you wait till later," the nurse replied. "He really needs to be kept quiet. Why don't you come later this afternoon?"

"What did they say?" Marnie asked, her eyes scanning Amy's face.

Amy told her. "I'm definitely *not* going to school," she said.

"But it'll keep your mind off worrying," Marnie said. She must have seen the uncertainty on Amy's face. "Look, if there's any news, I'll phone the school right away," she promised. "If I don't hear anything, then I'll come to pick you up after school and we can go straight to the hospital."

Amy reluctantly gave in. In a sense, she knew that Marnie was right. She would only think about Grandpa and Lou all day if she were at home.

Marnie gave Amy a ride to school. "I promise I'll call if the hospital calls," she said as Amy got out of the car. "Try not to worry."

Amy walked slowly into the school. She was so wrapped up in her own thoughts that she hardly noticed Ashley and Jade standing nearby.

"Hi, Amy," Ashley said, following her. "How's that foal coming along?" She probed. "Have you gotten her to lead yet?" Since she had lost interest in Ben, Ashley had dropped all pretense of being nice to Amy. "Or is she still standing in the middle of the field?"

Amy stopped. For a moment the insult made her temper rise, but as she looked into Ashley's taunting face, she suddenly didn't care. "Yeah, whatever, Ashley," she said flatly as she walked on. But not before she had caught the look of triumph in Ashley's eyes. She ignored it. Right now, she didn't have the energy for a fight. Walking around the corner, she almost bumped into Matt.

"Amy!" he exclaimed. "How are you? Scott told me about your grandpa being in the hospital. I'm really sorry."

"Thanks," Amy said briefly, walking on.

"Look," Matt said following her. "I'm sorry about what I said on Monday. I shouldn't have taken it all out on you."

"It doesn't really matter," Amy said flatly. "Just forget it."

Matt looked hurt. "I'm trying to apologize, Amy. I don't see why our friendship should suffer just because I'm dating Ashley."

Amy stopped and stared at him. "You're *dating* her?"

"Yeah," Matt admitted awkwardly. "Look, I know how you feel about Ashley," he said quickly, "but if you just spent some time with her —"

"Spend time with Ashley!" Amy exclaimed, feeling nothing but frustration. How could he think spending time with Ashley was even a possibility? "Get real, Matt! That's the last thing I'd want to do."

"Amy —" Matt said, stepping forward.

Amy shook her head. "Look, if you want to go out with Ashley, that's fine. Go ahead. Just don't expect me to be friends with her as well." And with that she swung her backpack onto her shoulder and marched away.

For the rest of the day, Matt avoided Amy. The sight of Ashley's hand resting possessively on Matt's arm at lunch made Amy so annoyed that it reinforced her initial disgust. She felt completely betrayed. Matt *knew* she couldn't stand Ashley. How could he even think about dating her?

As soon as school finished, she grabbed her books and set off at a run. Marnie was already parked on the road outside the school, ready to take her to the hospital.

"Relax," she said as Amy pulled open the car door. "I called the hospital before I left. They said it's OK to visit. Your grandpa's not any worse."

Amy felt a wave of relief rush over her. "Thanks, Marnie," she said. "Has Lou called?"

Marnie shook her head. "No."

Wondering whether that was good or bad, Amy sat back as Marnie drove through the traffic to the hospital. When they got there, Marnie suggested she wait in the reception area for Amy in case having two visitors tired Jack out.

Amy went nervously to Grandpa's room on her own. It quickly became clear that his condition might not be any worse, but it wasn't any better, either. His breathing was short and shallow, and every so often he reached for the mask at the side of the bed to get a boost of oxygen to his lungs.

"You don't sound too good, Grandpa," Amy said from the doorway as he coughed painfully.

"The doctor says it's just a small setback," Grandpa

wheezed. "Nothing to worry about. Is there any news from Lou?"

Amy shook her head. "Not yet."

"I guess she'll phone tonight," Grandpa said. He took a deep breath. "Well, tell me about you. How was school?"

Amy sat down next to him and told him a little about her classes and then started talking about the horses, hoping that if she kept talking, Grandpa wouldn't try to say anything. He listened and nodded. "And Marnie's settling in?" he said as Amy paused for breath.

"Yeah, she's great," Amy said. "She's been helping Ty and Ben today while I've been at school."

"Good," Grandpa said, looking relieved. "So you're all managing?"

"Yes," Amy told him firmly. She squeezed his hand. "You shouldn't worry about us, Grandpa. You just think about getting better."

🐛

When Amy and Marnie returned to Heartland, they found Scott there. "I just dropped by with a birthday present for Ty for tomorrow," he said as Amy jumped out of the car and walked over to him. "How's your grandpa?"

"He's not doing all that well," Amy admitted, realizing

that she'd totally forgotten it was Ty's birthday the next day. It was a good thing she'd ordered him a gift that day at the mall, and it had been delivered to Heartland already wrapped.

"Well, send Jack my best wishes," Scott said. "I'll stop by and visit him when he's feeling up to it."

Just then, Marnie came over. "Hi, Scott," she said warmly. "It's nice to see you again."

"You, too, Marnie," Scott smiled. He opened the car door to get in but stopped. "So, have you heard from Lou?" he asked casually.

"She called last night," Amy replied. "Didn't she call you, too?" As soon as the question left her lips, she couldn't believe she said it.

Scott's mouth tightened slightly. "No," he said.

"She sounded really tired," Amy stammered quickly. "She'll probably be in touch tonight or tomorrow."

"Yeah, maybe," Scott said, but he sounded as if he didn't quite believe her.

Amy suddenly remembered that his alumni dinner was scheduled for the next evening. "Are you still going to the reunion at your old vet school?" she asked.

Scott nodded.

"Oh, your reunion is tomorrow?" Marnie asked.

Scott explained about the dinner. "It's black tie. All very formal."

"It sounds kind of fun," Marnie said.

"You think?" Scott said.

"Sure," Marnie said. "I love things like that."

Scott frowned. "What would you think about coming with me?"

Marnie's eyes widened in surprise. "Really?"

"Yeah, I've still got Lou's ticket, and if you want to use it you're more than welcome," Scott replied. "It would be a lot more fun than going on my own."

"Well, if you're sure," Marnie said, beaming. She turned to Amy. "You'll be all right on your own tomorrow evening, won't you?"

"Of course I will," Amy said. "You go."

Scott smiled at Marnie. "Then in that case, I'd be honored if you'll be my date. I'll pick you up at seven." Getting into his Jeep, he drove away.

Marnie looked stunned. "Wow!" she said to Amy. "I wasn't expecting that." She glanced at her watch. "If I'm quick I'll just have time to get into town to find something to wear." She headed back to her car. "I'll be back in time to make dinner."

"See you," Amy called after her.

As Marnie turned the car around and drove off, Ty came across the yard.

"What's going on?" he asked, surprised. "Where's Marnie going?"

"Scott's invited her to his vet reunion dinner tomorrow," Amy told him. "So she's buying something to wear."

"How is Jack doing?" Ty asked.

Amy quickly filled him in. "He says it's just a setback, but he didn't look good. It seemed to hurt him to talk — even to breathe." She looked into Ty's familiar, understanding face and suddenly felt the urge to confide the fears she had been having since leaving the hospital, fears that she hadn't even admitted to Marnie. "You know what he's like, Ty, he'll never admit that there's anything wrong. I just hope he's not keeping something from me."

"You didn't see a doctor?" Ty said.

Amy shook her head. "They were all busy."

"Well, make sure you talk to one tomorrow," Ty said.

"I will," Amy sighed. Just then the phone rang. "That might be Lou!" she exclaimed.

She ran to the kitchen. "Heartland, Amy Fleming speaking."

"Hi, Amy, it's me."

"Lou!" Amy sat down with the phone, her heart starting to pound. "How are you? What's happened? Have you seen Daddy?"

"No," Lou said, sounding very disappointed. "I went to the address but it's not Daddy's house, it belongs to some friends of his. A neighbor I spoke to said that the family who lives there, the Carters, are away until Saturday. She also told me that Daddy had been staying with the Carters for a while but she didn't know where he is now."

"I don't get it," Amy said, confused. "Why did Daddy leave that address at the hotel then?"

Lou sighed. "I don't know."

"There must be some way of finding out where he is," Amy said, hating to hear Lou sounding so miserable. "Maybe these people — the Carters — will be able to tell you where he lives when they get home. I mean, he could have just been staying with them while his house was being remodeled or something."

"I guess," Lou said.

"You'd only have to wait two more days," Amy told her, trying to cheer her up.

"Yeah, you're right," Lou replied. "I'll find somewhere around here to stay and go to see the Carters on Saturday. How's Grandpa?" she asked anxiously.

"He's doing just fine," Amy lied, hoping it was the right thing to say. Lou sounded so down she couldn't tell her about Grandpa's setback.

"That's good," Lou said. "Is Marnie there? Can I talk to her?"

"Actually, she's out," Amy said.

"Out?" Lou echoed.

Amy hesitated, suddenly wondering how Lou would

take the news. "Yes. She's, um, gone out shopping for an outfit. Scott's invited her to that dinner tomorrow."

There was a silence on the other end of the line.

"It's just as friends," Amy said quickly, in case Lou was getting the wrong idea. "I mean, you know Marnie and Scott would never —"

"I know," Lou broke in. There was a pause. When she spoke again, her voice was flat. "Well, I'd better go. Tell Marnie that I hope she has a good time tomorrow. I'm glad Scott will have someone fun to go with."

"I'll tell her," Amy promised.

When Amy walked out of the house, she found Ty waiting for her. "Was it Lou?" he asked.

"Yep," Amy said.

"So?" Ty prompted, when she didn't say anything more. "Did she see your father?"

Amy told him what had happened. "She sounded so disappointed," she said to Ty. "I wish I could do something."

"Well, you can't. You're doing all you can," Ty said gently. His eyes searched hers. "Look, you shouldn't be on your own tomorrow night," he said suddenly. "How about I come over and we can cook dinner?"

"But it's your birthday!" Amy said. "Don't you want to go out?"

"I can go out anytime. And my family isn't celebrating until Sunday."

"But —" Amy began.

"No buts," Ty interrupted. "It's decided. I'll stay and keep you company tomorrow night until Marnie gets back."

He looked so determined that Amy gave in. "OK," she smiled gratefully. "Thanks."

Chapter Nine

When Amy woke up the next morning, the air had a strange, silent feel to it. Jumping out of bed, she went to the window. It had snowed heavily in the night, and the yard and the fields were covered in a thick white blanket. Everywhere looked very bleak.

"I'm not going to school today," Amy told Marnie when she went downstairs. "Now that it's snowed there's going to be loads to do in the yard, and I don't want to wait until this afternoon to see Grandpa."

Marnie took one look at her steadfast face and seemed to realize that there was no point in trying to argue. "OK," she said. "I'm not going to force you. But you will go back on Monday, won't you?"

Amy nodded and pulled on her boots. Right now

school just seemed so unimportant, but she guessed she couldn't stay away forever.

She went outside to give the horses their breakfast. As she fed Melody, she heard a muffled cough come from the back of the stall. She looked carefully at the foal and could see that Daybreak's nose was still running and her eyes looked dull. She checked the foal's temperature. It was normal, but Amy made a mental note to call Scott if the filly didn't seem any better by the following day.

Ty and Ben arrived and they all got to work. The snow meant that there were a lot of extra chores to do — ice in the water troughs to be broken, extra straw to put down on the horses' beds, the paths to be shoveled. Amy hurried around, trying not to think about Grandpa and Lou, just hoping to keep things going.

When Amy visited Grandpa later she forced herself to be as cheerful as possible so that he wouldn't worry. "How are things?" he wheezed.

"Everything's just fine," Amy told him.

Grandpa studied her with concern. "You're looking tired, honey."

"Me? No, I'm all right," Amy said, smiling and trying to look wide awake. "Lou called last night," she said, changing the subject quickly. "She sent her love."

Jack took a sip of water from the glass by his bedside. "Has she been able to talk with your father yet?"

"No, she went to the address, but it isn't Daddy's house," Amy replied. "It just belongs to some friends of his, and they're away until Saturday. She's hoping to see them then to find out where he's living."

For a moment Grandpa didn't speak. "I hope she's doing the right thing. I don't want to see her hurt," he said at last.

Amy decided not to tell him how unhappy Lou had sounded on the phone. "I'm sure she's fine," she said, wishing she could believe it.

When Amy got back to Heartland she immediately went back to work. There was something soothing about working. It meant she didn't have to think.

At half past six, Amy and Ty turned off the stable lights and went into the house. They had just gotten out some cookbooks and were arguing about what to eat for supper when Marnie came downstairs. "Well, what do you think?" she demanded, appearing in the doorway.

"You look amazing!" Amy exclaimed.

It was true. Marnie was wearing a long black evening dress. It had a low back, and the neckline and straps were intricately beaded with delicate crystals. Her wild blond hair was wrapped up in a tight bun, and she was wearing high-heeled, strappy shoes.

"Well," Ty said. "You're certainly not dressed to hang out with us."

Marnie grinned. "Well, I wanted to look my best. Just think of all the young vets who'll be there. If I find a good one, we can double-date with Scott and Lou."

Just then Scott beeped his horn outside. "See you later," Marnie said, going to the door.

"Bye!" Ty and Amy called together.

As the door shut behind her, Ty grinned. "I hope they have a good time. Now," he said, turning back to a cookbook on the kitchen table, "what do you mean, you don't like eggplant?"

"I just don't," Amy said. "Can't we have" — she pulled the book away from him — "farmhouse chicken casserole?"

"Too boring," Ty said. He stood up. "No, it looks like I'm just going to have to cook you my specialty."

"I'm afraid to ask what it is," Amy said dubiously.

"You'll have to wait and see," Ty said. "You should go upstairs and get changed, and I'll start cooking."

"I'm glad it's not your birthday every day — it makes you very bossy," Amy teased. But as she went upstairs she couldn't help feeling glad that he had insisted on staying.

When she came downstairs, Ty was busy frying some bacon.

"What can I do to help?" Amy asked.

"You can peel those potatoes," Ty said, nodding to a bag he'd put on the table. "Then they need slicing." Amy grabbed a peeler and a bowl of water and set to work.

As they worked, they chatted about the horses.

"Daybreak's been coughing a little today," Ty said after a bit. "And her nose is still running."

"Yeah, I noticed that, too," Amy said. "I thought I might call Scott tomorrow and get him to take a look at her."

Just then the phone rang. Amy picked up the receiver.

It was Lou. "How's Grandpa?" she asked.

"He's doing just fine," Amy lied. "How are you?"

Lou sighed. "OK, I suppose." She paused. "It's — it's just strange. England seems so different." She forced a laugh. "I've always thought of it as my home, but suddenly it doesn't seem like that anymore. Maybe it's because it's almost Christmas, but I can't stop thinking about all of you. I'm really missing everyone. I just keep wondering whether coming over here was a big mistake."

Amy heard the unhappiness in her sister's voice. "Of course it wasn't," she said firmly. "You'll meet the Carters tomorrow, they'll tell you where Daddy is, and then you'll be able to go and see him. It's all going to be worth it in the end."

"I suppose so," Lou said. She sighed. "Still, right now, I wish I was there with you."

As Amy put the phone down, Ty looked at her. "What's the matter?" he asked, looking at her face.

"It's just more of the same," Amy said, sitting down. "Lou's feeling down." She shook her head. "I wish there was something I could do to help."

Ty looked at her sympathetically. "She'll be back soon."

Amy nodded. "Yeah."

"Come on, cheer up," Ty said softly. He crouched beside her, taking her hands. "You've got to stop taking on everyone's worries. You're being too hard on yourself."

Amy looked down into his familiar green eyes, and for a moment it was as though she was seeing his face for the first time. Her gaze followed the sweep of his cheekbones down to his serious, sensitive mouth. Meeting his eyes again, she saw a warmth just like there had been the night of the Grants' party. Feeling herself blush, Amy jumped to her feet.

"I haven't given you your birthday present yet," she stammered. "I'll get it."

She ran up the stairs, her heart pounding and her palms damp. What was the matter with her?

Reaching her bedroom, she picked up the gift from her dressing table. Forcing herself to stop, she took a few deep breaths. *It was just the stress of everything,* she told herself. She was overreacting. All Ty had done was hold her hands and try to reassure her. But as she shut her eyes, the image of his face forced itself into her mind. It was the way his eyes had looked at her — so deep and so searching.

Looking in the mirror, she saw that her cheeks were still flushed. She took another few deep breaths to calm down and then went back downstairs with the gift.

Ty was setting the table. "Here," Amy said, holding out the box and the card she had gotten him. "There's a card and present from Lou and Grandpa as well," she said.

Ty opened the cards first and then Lou and Grandpa's gift — a new riding hat and a pair of gloves.

"Wow," Ty said, "these are great!"

"Now open mine," Amy said, eager to see what he would think of the present she had bought for him.

Ty picked up the package and began to open it. Amy watched his face as he took out her gift, a leather-bound book on herbal remedies for horses signed by the author, George Verrall. She knew Ty had been wanting it for ages, and she had requested the mall bookstore to special order it.

"Look inside," she said eagerly as Ty took the book out of the gift wrap. Below George Verrall's signature Amy had written her mom's words: *By healing, we heal ourselves.*

"Do you like it?" she asked anxiously as Ty read the words.

"This is something I've always wanted," Ty said softly, touching the quotation with his forefinger and looking at her. "Thank you."

Amy was so relieved he liked the gift, she couldn't stop smiling. For a moment the two of them just stared at each other. Almost before Amy knew what was happening, Ty stepped forward and his arms seemed to fold around her.

Suddenly, the phone rang.

Amy and Ty broke apart. Amy darted across the kitchen and grabbed the hand set. "Heartland," she stammered. "Amy Fleming speaking."

An efficient voice spoke on the other end. "Hello, Amy, this is Dr. Marshall at Meadowville Park Hospital. I'm glad I reached you."

Amy's heart skipped a beat. "Dr. Marshall," she echoed. "Is it Grandpa? Is he all right?"

There was a slight pause. "I'm afraid I've got some troubling news," Dr. Marshall said gently.

Amy felt her insides turn to ice. "What is it?"

"Your grandfather's condition has deteriorated in the last few hours," Dr. Marshall replied. "One of his lungs has collapsed. He's now in Intensive Care. I think you had better come to the hospital right away."

Chapter Ten

Ty was beside Amy even before she had put the phone down. "Was that the hospital?" he demanded. "What's wrong?"

Amy started to shake. "It's Grandpa," she whispered, so distraught that she could barely get the words out. "He's been moved to Intensive Care. I've got to go. I have to be with him."

Not stopping to ask any more questions, Ty grabbed their coats from the back of the door. "Come on," he said, handing Amy her jacket. "I'll drive you."

Moving automatically, Amy pulled her jacket on. "What about Marnie?" she said suddenly. "She'll wonder where we are."

"I'll leave her a note to tell her we're at the hospital," Ty said. He tore a piece of paper from the notebook by the phone and scribbled a message. He left it in an obvious place on the table and turned off the oven. "Let's go."

Too scared to think straight, Amy followed him out of the house. A light snow was falling, but she hardly even noticed as the flakes caught in her hair. She got into the pickup and huddled against the cold seat. Ty turned the key and the engine rumbled into life.

"So what did the hospital say?" Ty asked, swinging the truck around and setting off down the driveway.

"One of Grandpa's lungs has collapsed." Amy's teeth began to chatter.

Ty looked at her with concern. "Here," he said, pulling a travel blanket out from beneath the seat and tossing it to her. "You're in shock."

Amy wrapped the blanket around herself, but neither it nor the roaring heater could stop her from shivering. At the first set of traffic signals, Ty stopped, rummaged in the glove compartment, and pulled out a small brown bottle with a dropper in the top. "Bach Flower Rescue Remedy," he said softly, handing it to her. "It's not just for horses. Put four drops under your tongue."

Amy did what he said. All she could think about was Grandpa. A collapsed lung sounded so critical. What if he didn't get better?

Oh, please, she prayed desperately as the wheels of the

truck cut through the slush on the roads and the lights of the late-night stores flashed past. *I'll do anything. Please just let Grandpa get better.*

❧

The half-hour journey to the hospital seemed to take forever, but at last Ty pulled up in the empty visitors' parking lot outside the sprawling complex of low white buildings. Once in the hospital, they were shown into a small room, and a few minutes later Dr. Marshall joined them.

"How's my grandpa?" Amy asked, jumping to her feet.

"His condition's very serious," Dr. Marshall said gravely.

"Will he be OK?" Amy whispered.

"Collapsed lungs aren't usually life-threatening, providing treatment is administered quickly," Dr. Marshall replied. "However, in your grandfather's case, there have been complications."

"Complications?" Amy echoed.

"He has what is known as a tension pneumothorax, which means that the air can't escape properly from his good lung," the doctor explained. "It's potentially fatal. Now that doesn't mean he's going to die," she added quickly, seeing Amy's face. "We've stabilized his condition. But I have to tell you the next few hours will be critical."

"Can I see him?" Amy asked, hardly able to get the words out.

Dr. Marshall nodded. "He's sedated at the moment, but yes, you can see him."

Amy and Ty followed the doctor down the corridors. When they reached the Intensive Care Unit, Dr. Marshall opened the door.

Grandpa was lying immobile on the hospital bed, his eyes shut. Tubes led into his nose, chest, and wrist, and beside the bed several machines blinked and whirred. A nurse was bustling around. Seeing Amy, she looked at her sympathetically. "Are you Mr. Bartlett's granddaughter?"

Amy nodded, her eyes on the still figure. She felt Ty's hand squeeze her shoulder, and as the nurse moved out of the way, she went over to the bed. Grandpa's skin was very pale and he hardly looked like himself.

Swallowing hard, Amy sat down on the chair beside the bed and put her hand over one of Grandpa's. It was cold and clammy and motionless.

"We'll leave you for a few moments," Dr. Marshall said. "If there's any problem, just press the red button on the wall."

The door shut behind the doctor and nurse.

"Do you want me to stay, or do you want to be on your own?" Ty asked softly.

Amy looked up at him. "Stay — please." She turned to Grandpa again. "I just can't bear to see him like this."

Ty put his arm around her shoulders. "It'll be OK, Amy."

"First Mom and then Pegasus and now —" She bit her lip, struggling not to give way to the familiar anguish that was threatening to overwhelm her again. She bent her head, her long hair falling across her face. "I love him so much."

"And he loves you," Ty said, crouching beside her, his eyes intense. "Come on, you know what your grandpa's like. He won't give up. He's a fighter."

Amy swallowed, knowing Ty was right. "Grandpa, can you hear me?" she whispered, clutching her grandfather's limp hand. "You've got to fight — please, do it for me. Please fight."

❧

The long hours of the night slowly passed. Amy hardly moved from Grandpa's bedside. Just after two o'clock in the morning, Scott and Marnie appeared at the door of the Intensive Care Unit.

"Amy," Marnie whispered. "We came as soon as we saw the note."

Pulling away from Grandpa, she went to the doorway and hugged them both.

"Does Lou know?" Scott asked.

Amy shook her head bleakly. "I don't know where she is."

Scott cursed under his breath.

Amy glanced at the door. She didn't want to be away from Grandpa for even a second. "I'm going back in."

Leaving Ty to explain exactly what had happened, she returned to Grandpa's side.

After ten minutes, Ty returned. "Marnie's offered to stay here with you," he said. "I'm going to go back to Heartland so that I can feed the horses in the morning. Ben should probably know, too. Is it OK if I tell him?"

Amy nodded. She didn't want Ty to go, but she knew that it made sense. Marnie didn't know enough about the horses to handle the morning feeds, and Ty was right, Ben needed to know what was going on.

"It'll mean someone will be there if Lou calls, too," Ty said. "You'll be all right with Marnie, won't you?"

"Yeah," Amy said. She forced her lips into a smile and stood up. "Thanks, Ty."

"No problem," Ty said. "I'll see you soon." He hugged her for a moment, then left.

Marnie sat with Amy through the remainder of that long night. They talked a little but mainly sat in silence as the hours ticked by. Amy was glad for the quiet. Her mind felt as if it had shut down, as if all normal actions like speaking and smiling were beyond her. All she wanted was for Grandpa to open his eyes and speak to her, to show her that he was going to get better.

She remembered the hours she had spent with him when she had been too little to help her mom in the stables — helping him clean the house, weed the vegetable garden, do the grocery shopping. All the games he'd played with her. She remembered how he had always been there for her when Mom was too busy. Grandpa had been the one who listened when she wanted to talk, who helped her with her school projects.

As she looked at his lined face lying against the pillow, she realized that he had grown older without her noticing. He always had such energy that she had never really thought of him as old, but now her gaze traced the deep grooves on his forehead, the wrinkles around his eyes. She and Lou should have insisted that he take things easier.

As the gray light of dawn streaked across the dark sky, she scooted her chair forward and put a hand to his face, trying to imagine what life would be like without him. "Grandpa," she whispered. "I love you."

Her hand froze. She was sure his eyelids had moved. Had she imagined it?

"Grandpa?" she said.

This time she knew there was no mistake. He blinked.

His lips moved but his voice barely made a sound. "Amy?"

"Yes, Grandpa!" Amy gasped. "It's me!"

Behind her, she heard Marnie jump to her feet. "I'll get a doctor."

Amy barely registered the sound of the door opening and shutting. Grandpa's eyes blinked open again. "Throat's dry . . . water . . ." he croaked.

"The doctor will be here in a minute," Amy told him, clutching his hand, silently praying that Grandpa was now going to be OK.

Over the next half hour, a succession of doctors and nurses hurried in and out of Jack's room, until at last Amy was left alone with him again. He was still attached to all the tubes, and his face was still pale, but at least he was awake.

Amy kissed him gently on the cheek. "I was so worried about you, Grandpa," she said.

Jack spoke slowly, every breath an effort. "It'll take more than a bit of pneumonia to get rid of me," he whispered. He covered her hand with his. "You look tired, honey. What time is it?"

"It's early in the morning. I've been here all night, but I'm OK."

"Lou —" Jack began.

"As soon as she calls I'll tell her what's happened," Amy said quickly. "She'll be back in no time, Grandpa."

"No," Grandpa wheezed. "Don't worry her. I don't want her to come back just for me. Make her stay until she's seen your father."

"But, Grandpa," Amy began, "she'll want to be here. She'll —"

"No, Amy," Jack said weakly. His words were slow, but his tone was insistent. "I stopped her from seeing your father before. I'm not going to be the one to stop her again. Please, promise me you'll make her stay."

Amy stared at him. How *could* she promise that? But then she couldn't bear to see the distress in Grandpa's eyes. "I'll try," she agreed reluctantly.

"Thank you," Grandpa said, the words no more than a whisper as he sank back against the pillows.

"I'd better go," Amy said, "but I'll be back later. You get some rest now, Grandpa."

He nodded and closed his eyes. Amy heard him sigh with relief as he drifted off to sleep.

❧

Amy followed Marnie out of the hospital and into the parking lot. It had stopped snowing now, but the heavy morning clouds seemed to promise that there was more to come. The freezing air hit Amy's face like a splash of icy water, but instead of making her feel more awake it seemed to have the opposite effect. The adrenaline that had been surging through her body over the last fourteen hours suddenly drained out of her and all her muscles turned to lead. Getting into Marnie's car, she leaned her head heavily against the window.

"I think it's bed for us when we get back," Marnie said, starting the engine.

As Marnie drove home, Amy blinked hard to stop her eyes from shutting. She looked at Marnie. Her blond curls had long since escaped from the bun, and her evening dress was creased and rumpled. "Thanks for staying with me, Marnie," Amy said gratefully.

Marnie turned her tired eyes to her and smiled. "That's what friends are for. I couldn't have left you there on your own." She yawned. "I'm just glad Jack's getting better."

When they reached Heartland, Ty and Ben came hurrying to meet them.

"How's Jack?" Ty asked.

"Still improving," Marnie said.

Amy noticed the dark shadows beneath Ty's eyes. He looked as if he'd hardly slept. "Has Lou called?" she asked.

Ty shook his head.

"Come on," Ben said, leading the way to the house.

"We've got some coffee on, and you both look like you could use some breakfast."

They followed him into the house. Once in the kitchen, Amy collapsed onto a chair at the table and let her head rest on her arms.

Her mind was just starting to swim toward sleep when she felt Marnie's hand on her shoulder. "Go to bed," Marnie said gently. "You can eat later. Right now you need rest."

Amy fell into bed and slept for six straight hours. When she woke up, daylight was streaming in through her window. She looked around in confusion. What was she doing in bed? Gradually the events of the last twenty-four hours came rolling back. Grandpa. The hospital . . .

Jumping out of bed, she went downstairs. The kitchen was deserted. Picking up the phone, she dialed the hospital. Dr. Marshall had gone off duty, but one of her colleagues came to the phone to speak to Amy.

"Your grandfather's doing well," he said reassuringly. "His lung has stabilized, and providing all goes well the damage should now start to heal. We'll need to monitor his condition very carefully over the next week. In this sort of case, there's always the danger that the lung could collapse again. If that happens, then we'll be looking at major surgery. However, such relapses are rare, and we're hopeful that your grandfather will make a rapid and full recovery."

Feeling comforted by the doctor's words, Amy replaced the receiver. As she did so, her gaze fell on Ty's birthday presents. They had been piled up on the dresser, forgotten in the drama of the night before. The sight of them brought a vivid memory flashing into Amy's mind — Ty's arms wrapping around her, his eyes looking into her own.

The back door opened. Amy jumped and swung around. It was Ty.

"Ty," Amy stammered, acutely aware of what she'd just been thinking.

Ty didn't seem to notice her confusion. "I was just coming in to leave you a note," he said, rubbing a weary hand across his eyes. "Ben offered to finish the work, so I thought I'd head home and get some sleep. If that's OK."

"Of course," Amy said. "You've got to be exhausted."

Ty forced a smile. "I'm a little tired. Have you talked to the hospital?"

"Yeah." Amy told him what the doctor had said. "He sounded pleased with Grandpa's progress," she finished.

"Good," Ty said, looking relieved. "Well, I'll see you tomorrow then."

"Don't forget your birthday presents," Amy said quickly as he turned to go.

Ty glanced at the dresser and then he looked at her. From the suddenly guarded look on his face, Amy was sure that he, too, was thinking about the night before. She caught her breath, thinking that he was about to say something, but then in a split second he seemed to change his mind and the tension left his face.

"Thanks for reminding me," he said, going to the dresser and picking up his gifts. When he turned to Amy again, his eyes showed nothing more than genuine concern. "Look, if you need me for anything, just give me a call."

Not trusting herself to speak, Amy nodded.

As the door closed behind him she sank down on a chair, feeling confused and mixed up. Her thoughts whirled. There was so much to think about. Grandpa, Lou, Ty . . . She put her head in her hands. It was all getting to be too much.

Hearing footsteps on the stairs, she looked up as Marnie came into the kitchen. "I thought I heard you down here," Marnie said, yawning. "Is there any news from the hospital?"

Quickly pulling herself together, Amy filled Marnie in on her conversation with the doctor. Just as she was finishing, the phone rang.

"Hi, Amy." It was Lou. Her voice sounded shaky.

"Lou!" Amy exclaimed, glancing at Marnie in relief.

"I'm so glad you've called. It's — " But before she could finish, Lou broke in.

"Oh, Amy," she said, bursting into tears.

For a second, Amy was almost too shocked to speak. Lou never cried. "Lou!" she said in alarm. "What happened?"

"It's Daddy," Lou sobbed.

Horrible thoughts raced through Amy's mind. Daddy! Was he injured? Dead? "What's the matter?" she said quickly. "He's not — "

"No," Lou said, seeming to read her thoughts. "He's OK. It's just — just — he's not even here. He's in Australia."

"Australia!" Amy echoed, astounded. "What's he doing there?"

"He lives there," Lou said.

Amy began to feel that she was losing her grip on the conversation. "What do you mean?"

"I went to see the Carters today," Lou explained, sounding like she was struggling to control herself. "Michael Carter is not just friends with Daddy, he's his business partner as well. They have a company that specializes in importing and exporting horses between England and Australia. He told me that when Daddy's over here he stays with them but that he actually lives in Australia."

"But Daddy never said anything about Australia in his letter," Amy said, trying to get her head around what Lou was saying.

"I can't believe I've come all this way for nothing," Lou said.

Amy didn't know what to say. She understood the disappointment Lou must be feeling — to have psyched herself up for meeting their father only to find he was thousands of miles away.

"You'll get to see him soon," Amy said, trying to comfort her.

"But I've been so stupid," Lou sniffed. "I should never have left Heartland. Especially with Grandpa being ill and everything. How is he today?"

Amy paused. The last thing she wanted was to make Lou feel worse, but she knew she had to tell her the truth. "Um . . . he's not good, Lou," she said. She took a deep breath. "One of his lungs collapsed last night."

Lou gasped. Amy quickly explained what had happened.

"What am I going to do?" Lou said in an anguished voice. "I need to see him. I'm coming home," Lou said with determination. "I'm going to change my flight tomorrow, get the first seat out I can." She swallowed hard. "Tell Grandpa I love him, Amy."

When Amy replaced the receiver, she stood by the phone feeling stunned.

"What's the news?" Marnie asked anxiously.

Amy told her.

"Poor Lou," Marnie said, aghast.

"I wish she was here, Marnie," Amy said.

Marnie put an arm around her shoulders. "Don't worry," she said, hugging her. "She'll be back soon."

✥

After supper Amy and Marnie returned to the hospital. Grandpa was awake when they arrived. He was still connected to the various tubes and machines, but Amy was relieved to see that some color had returned to his face. She decided to keep the truth about Lou and Daddy for when he had recovered some more.

When Amy and Marnie got back to Heartland, Marnie announced that she was going to go to bed. "You look like you could use some sleep, too," she said to Amy.

But Amy's mind was buzzing with thoughts of Grandpa, Lou, and Daddy. "I think I'll stay up for a bit," she said, sitting down in an armchair and picking up the remote control. "I'll watch TV."

"Do you want some company?" Marnie asked her.

Amy shook her head. "No, I'll be fine. You should go to bed."

"Night, then," Marnie said, and she went upstairs.

Amy flicked through the channels and eventually

settled on a sitcom. By ten-thirty she was almost asleep in the chair. Yawning widely, she got to her feet and turned the TV off. She went to the kitchen window. Apart from the lights on the front stable block, everywhere was dark. She was about to go upstairs to bed when she hesitated. For some reason, she felt that something wasn't right. She glanced outside again. Everything seemed quiet enough, but still she felt a nagging urge to go and check.

With a sigh, she pulled on her jacket and boots. She knew she wouldn't be able to relax until she had looked around the yard and checked that everything really was OK.

She went out into the darkness. As she walked toward the barns she thought about Lou. She hoped her sister could get an early flight. It would be wonderful to have her home again.

The top doors of the stalls in the stable block were all shut. Amy opened each one and checked inside, but all the horses appeared to be happy and content.

She turned and trudged through the snow to the back barn. Pulling back the door, she slipped inside and pressed the light switch. There were a few startled snorts from the stalls as the lights flickered on but nothing out of the ordinary. Still, Amy walked down the aisle, checking over each stall door. Dancer, Sundance, Jasmine . . .

She reached Daybreak and Melody's stall. The mare was pulling at her hay net, and the little filly was standing beside her. Amy was about to move on to the next stall when she paused. Daybreak was standing unusually still, her sides visibly moving in and out.

Feeling a sudden prickle of worry run down her spine, Amy pushed back the bolt on the door. Melody looked around but Daybreak didn't. Lowering her head, the foal coughed. Amy went over. For once, Daybreak didn't try to move away. She stood submissively as Amy gently felt her glands. They were swollen. With mounting concern, Amy noticed that the filly had a thick yellow discharge running from her nose and that her eyes were dull. There was no doubt about it, Daybreak was ill — possibly very ill.

Chapter Eleven

"Equine herpes virus," Scott said an hour later as he stepped back from examining Daybreak. "I'm sure of it." He patted the foal. "But I'll still need to run a few tests to confirm it."

"What does that mean?" Marnie asked from where she stood in the doorway, with a coat on over her pajamas.

"It's a virus that causes respiratory infections," Scott replied. While Amy held Daybreak he took a blood sample and a sample of mucus from the foal's windpipe. "It particularly affects young horses," he went on. "At first the symptoms are mild — a clear nasal discharge, occasional cough, and possibly a rise in temperature. It doesn't look too serious at that point, but if left untreated a more serious secondary bacterial infection can develop. That's what's happened to Daybreak."

"But how would she have gotten it?" Amy asked.

"I imagine one of the other horses must have brought it to the yard," Scott said. "It generally doesn't affect adult horses to this degree so you probably haven't noticed it. Daybreak's been affected more severely because, at her age, she still has a relatively immature immune system." He looked at Amy. "Did you notice her nose running in the last week or so?"

"Yes," Amy said, feeling horribly guilty. "I was going to call you yesterday, but then with Grandpa at the hospital, I just forgot."

Scott nodded sympathetically. "That's understandable. You've had a lot going on. Well, don't worry. I think we've caught it early enough. Daybreak will need a course of antibiotics to control the secondary infection and some drugs to help break up the mucus in her lungs. Nursing is also very important if she's to recover quickly. She needs that liquid. She needs warmth and rest — keep her to just short lead walks each day. Here's the hard part. She needs to avoid dust. Do you think you could move her and Melody to one of the front stables so she can get more fresh air?"

"Yeah, we'll go work that out," Amy said.

"Keep the bedding deep and clean," Scott continued, "and try to see if she keeps feeding. I'll stop by tomorrow and vaccinate the other horses to stop the virus from spreading any further."

"OK. And should I use any herbs on her?" Amy asked.

Scott nodded. "Anything that will help her expel the mucus is ideal. You might want to try eucalyptus or tea tree oil."

He rummaged in his bag and took out a syringe and a bottle of antibiotics. After shaking the bottle, he filled the syringe and injected the antibiotics into Daybreak's hindquarters. "OK," he said. "I'll come back tomorrow morning and see how she's doing."

❧

It was past midnight when Scott left and Amy went into the tack room. Near the medicine cabinet was a shelf of books that had once belonged to her mom. She picked one on herbal remedies and began to leaf through the pages.

"You're not going to do anything more tonight, are you?" Marnie said, coming into the tack room.

Amy looked up. "I want to see if I can find anything to help her."

"But Amy, you're exhausted," Marnie said.

"I'm OK," Amy replied. She did feel incredibly tired, but she also felt incredibly guilty. How could she have forgotten about calling Scott? If she'd asked him to come a few days earlier maybe Daybreak wouldn't be so ill now. She saw Marnie's worried face. "I won't stay out long. I promise," she said. "But I'm not coming in just yet."

Her voice was so determined that Marnie had no choice but to give in. "All right," she said reluctantly. "But I'll make you some hot chocolate to keep you going."

Alone in the tack room, Amy ran her eyes over the pages on respiratory infections and herbal expectorants. Although garlic was highly recommended, the book suggested that it could upset the digestive system of young foals, so she decided to use echinacea roots instead. Echinacea, she read, had excellent antiviral and antibacterial qualities. It would stimulate the body to produce more white blood cells to fight the infection, and it could safely be used with antibiotics. She checked the dosage — ten grams of the cut root a day — and took some out of the cabinet. She also took out a bottle of eucalyptus oil and some cotton before returning to Daybreak's stall.

The little filly was still standing dejectedly beside Melody. Her head was hanging and her nose streamed. Her ears barely flickered as Amy looked over the door.

"It's all right," Amy told her softly. "You'll soon get better."

Marnie appeared with the hot drink for Amy and helped her bring a pitchfork and some fresh straw to make the bed clean and deep, like Scott had suggested.

Once the stall had been cleared and the new straw added, Amy crouched down beside Daybreak's head and encouraged her to eat the cut-up pieces of echinacea root. At first the filly simply mouthed it with her lips, but as soon as she tasted the plant she began to nibble on the pieces with more interest. It was almost as if she sensed they would help her.

When all the root was gone, Amy wiped Daybreak's nostrils with clean cotton and then poured a few drops of eucalyptus oil onto a fresh piece of cotton. Keeping the pad a few inches away from Daybreak's nostrils in case the concentrated oil irritated the foal's skin, Amy let Daybreak inhale the strong scent. She knew eucalyptus oil was supposed to be good for clearing blocked airways and loosening any infected mucus.

After a few minutes she decided that Daybreak had inhaled enough and she took the cotton away. As she took it over to the door, Daybreak lay down heavily in the straw. Amy went over and knelt beside the filly. "You're going to be OK," she murmured, stroking Daybreak's neck.

At her touch, the filly lifted her head slightly, a hint of her old spirit in her eyes, but she was too sick to really object. With a cough, she let her muzzle sink back heavily onto the straw. Amy looked at her for a long moment and then crept out of the stall.

A<small>S</small> soon as Amy got up the next morning, she pulled on her clothes and went straight to the barn, her head feeling dizzy from lack of sleep. Dawn had hardly broken and the freezing wind whipped her face. Winter was really closing in. The turnout paddocks looked bleak and cold, the thick layer of snow seeming to suffocate the ground.

"How are you, girl?" Amy said, her gloved fingers fumbling with the bolt on the stall door.

The little foal was standing beside her mother. Her breathing was just as fast and shallow as it had been the night before and her eyes were dull. She didn't look any better. Amy's heart sank. "We'd better get you cleaned up," she said, looking at the foal's streaming nose.

The other horses in the barn had seen Amy and had started to kick their doors and call expectantly for their breakfast. But for once Amy ignored them. Using cotton and warm water, she bathed Daybreak's nostrils and dried them thoroughly before offering the foal some eucalyptus oil to sniff again. Daybreak inhaled listlessly, her ears drooping. All the spirit seemed to have drained out of her.

When Ty and Ben arrived, she told them about Daybreak. A pained look crossed Ty's face. "I can't believe I didn't notice," he said. "I knew she wasn't well. I should have kept a closer eye on her."

"I should have noticed, too," Ben said. "I knew you were both distracted."

Even though Amy still felt guilty herself, she was too tired to waste energy on placing blame. "Look," she said wearily, "none of us noticed. Let's just leave it at that. Now we just need to try to get her better." She told them what Scott had said.

"She can have Red's stall," Ben offered immediately, heading for the door. "It's the biggest. I'll go get started on cleaning out his bed."

"Thanks, Ben," Amy said gratefully.

Ty was still angry with himself. "I can't believe I didn't notice," he said under his breath as Ben left. "I just forgot about her."

Amy sighed. "Ty, don't be so hard on yourself."

Ty looked at her. "But I should be making things easier for you."

Amy looked at him, too tired to smile. "You are," she said.

❧

Amy and Ty took turns monitoring the little filly until Scott arrived. He gave her another shot of antibiotics.

"Her temperature's still too high," he told them. "Is she feeding?"

Amy nodded. Daybreak wasn't feeding very hard or for very long, but she was still suckling.

Scott looked relieved. "Good. Let me know immediately if she stops. It's vital that she keeps it up. If she doesn't, she'll become dehydrated very quickly."

"We'll keep an eye on her," Ty promised.

Amy told Scott about the remedies she had been using. "Keep going," Scott said. "We need to do whatever we can to help her to fight this infection off as quickly as possible." He picked up his bag. "OK, let's go and vaccinate the other horses."

❧

Amy spent the rest of the day with the filly, only leaving her to visit Grandpa in the hospital. The tube to his nose had been removed, although a drip still ran into his arm and the chest tubes were still in place. He seemed a little more alert, but he told her that the doctors didn't think he would be able to leave hospital for another two weeks.

"But that means you won't be home for Christmas," Amy said, aghast.

"I'm afraid so, honey," Grandpa replied. "But you'll have Lou and Marnie for company and you can come visit." He squeezed her hand. "It won't be that bad."

It will! Amy wanted to cry, but seeing the worry on Grandpa's face she smiled as cheerfully as she could. "Of course we'll manage," she said, "but we'll miss you."

In the car on the way back to Heartland, Amy felt a tide of emotion threaten to overwhelm her. Her first Christmas without Mom, and now she wouldn't have Grandpa, either. *Oh, Lou*, she thought desperately, looking out the car window with tears stinging the back of her eyes, *please hurry home.*

❧

When Lou called that evening, she had more bad news. "I went to the airport but I couldn't get a flight," she told Amy. "The air traffic controllers over here are on strike, and it doesn't look like I'll be able to get back for a couple more days."

"But you have to!" Amy burst out, feeling a hard lump pressing in her throat. "Lou! I —" she caught the words "need you" just before they left her lips. Lou was upset enough already; she didn't need to be made to feel any worse. "Well, I guess it's only a few more days," Amy said, forcing herself to sound calm.

"But I don't want to wait," Lou said. "I want to come home."

"You'll be here soon," Amy said as brightly as she could.

The second she put the phone down though, the

brightness faded from her face and a wave of bleak misery engulfed her. She couldn't bear it.

A floorboard on the landing above creaked. Guessing that Marnie was coming down, Amy grabbed her jacket and ran outside. She simply couldn't pretend to be strong and cheerful for one second longer.

She ran to the front stable block, her breath coming in short bursts. Unbolting the door of Melody and Daybreak's new stall, she went in and, collapsing on the straw in the corner, she burst into tears.

She looked toward Daybreak lying beside Melody, her head resting on the straw, her breathing noisy. Amy remembered the night the filly had been born. Life had seemed so full of hope then.

"Amy?"

Amy looked up. Marnie was standing in the doorway of the stall, a horrified look in her eyes as she took in Amy's distraught face. "Amy, what's wrong?" She came over and knelt beside her. "What's happened?"

Amy knew that there was no way she could hide the truth from Marnie. "It's Lou," she cried. "And Grandpa and Daybreak and everything! I just can't deal with it anymore."

Marnie put her arms around her. "It's all right," she said soothingly. "I'm here. You don't have to deal with it alone. Now, tell me what's wrong. What's happened with Lou?"

"She can't get home," Amy said, and she told Marnie all about Lou's phone call. "She's so unhappy and there's nothing I can do to help her. I'm useless."

Marnie hugged her fiercely. "Amy, you've been wonderful," she said. "I've seen how cheerful you've been with your grandpa and how you've been trying so hard not to worry Lou. You've kept things going, and it's taken real courage." She shook her head. "I tell you, there's been such a big change in you since I was last here."

Amy looked up at her. "Really?" she asked, surprised at the statement.

"Really," Marnie said softly, her blue eyes searching Amy's face. "Your mom would have been proud of you, Amy. I know she would."

For a moment neither of them spoke.

"Look," Marnie said softly. "Don't worry about Christmas. We'll spend it with your Grandpa in the hospital, and if Lou's still in England, we'll call her every hour if it makes you happier. You shouldn't worry about Daybreak, either. She's going to get better. It'll just take a little while for the medicine and herbs to work, like it did with your grandpa." She squeezed Amy's arm. "Things will turn out OK, you'll see."

Amy nodded slowly.

Marnie hugged her again. "Come on, let's go back inside."

Amy hesitated. "I will," she said. "In a moment."

Marnie studied her face and then stood up. "OK," she said, seeming to sense Amy's need to be on her own. "But don't stay out here too long."

As Marnie's footsteps faded away, Amy leaned back against the stall wall. *Would Mom have been proud of me?* she wondered wearily. *I just don't know.*

She looked at Daybreak lying in the straw. The filly's sides heaved painfully in and out, and getting to her feet, Amy went over to her. Crouching down, she laid her hand on Daybreak's neck. Some of her old fire flared in the filly's eyes and she threw her head up, but the sudden movement made her cough painfully. With a heavy sigh, she let her muzzle sink back on the straw.

Amy began to massage the foal's neck with slow circular movements. When she felt Daybreak's muscles start to relax, she let her hands work up over the foal's neck and then, with a lighter pressure, over her delicate ears, face, and nose. Closing her own eyes, she focused completely on the instinctive movement of her fingers. As she breathed in the warm scent of horse and straw, the stress and tension of the last few days seemed to fade away. The world seemed to shrink until it contained nothing but her fingers and Daybreak's skin.

She wasn't sure how long she worked on the little filly, but when she finally opened her eyes she found that a feeling of peace had crept over her. She glanced at the foal's sides. Daybreak's breathing had slowed; the tension around her muzzle had relaxed. Her eyes were half shut.

Amy gently eased backward and stood up, her heart turning over as she looked at the little foal lying so still in the straw. With one last glance at Daybreak, she crept quietly out of the stall.

Chapter Twelve

Amy slept better that night. Although the things she had been worried about the evening before hadn't changed, the time in the stall with Daybreak had somehow calmed her, and she awoke with a new sense of strength. *I can cope,* she thought. *Christmas might not be perfect, but Grandpa and Daybreak will get better and Lou will be home sometime soon — I know she will.*

Downstairs, she found Marnie in the kitchen putting on some fresh coffee. "How are you feeling?" she asked.

"Good," Amy replied, and instead of it being just something she said automatically, she found that she really meant it. She smiled. "Yeah, I'm feeling good."

The first thing Amy did when she went out to the stables was to go to Daybreak and Melody's stall.

The little foal was still lying in the straw, but even from the door Amy could see that her breathing looked calmer. She went into the stall and crouched beside the filly. "Hi, little one," she said, reaching out to gently scratch Daybreak's neck.

At the touch of her hand, the foal lifted her head, but for once her eyes didn't fill with hostility. She stared at Amy for a moment, and then, turning her head, she sniffed the back of Amy's hand. Amy felt a flicker of surprise. "Good girl," she said, tickling Daybreak's muzzle.

As she did so, she noticed that the filly's eyes were brighter. Maybe she was finally beginning to get better.

Feeling much happier, Amy left the stall and went to start the feeds.

❧

She had just finished the feeding when Scott's Jeep came bumping up the drive. As he parked, Amy saw that he wasn't alone — Matt was with him.

"Hi," Scott said to Amy and Marnie as he and Matt jumped out of the Jeep. "How's the patient today?"

"A bit better, I think," Amy said.

"Good," Scott said. "That's what I want to hear."

As Scott got his bag from the backseat, Amy looked uncertainly at Matt. "Hi, Matt."

He smiled awkwardly. "Hi," he said. "Scott's giving me a ride to school. How are you?"

"OK, thanks," Amy replied.

There was a silence. The angry words they had exchanged the last time they'd met trembled in the air between them.

Scott walked over to them. "Should we go and see Daybreak?" he said. Not waiting for an answer, he headed to the stables. Marnie shot a curious look at Amy and Matt and then joined him.

Amy was about to follow when Matt caught hold of her arm. "Amy —" he said.

Amy stopped and looked at him.

"I really am sorry," Matt said. "About your grandpa and Daybreak and — and about the argument we had."

Amy nodded.

"Can't we make up?" Matt continued. "I don't want us to argue about who I'm dating. We've been friends for too long, and I don't want that to change."

"But why *Ashley*?" The words burst out of Amy. "I mean, of all the people in the world, Matt, why her?"

"I like her," Matt said simply. "Since Jade's been going out with Dan, I've really gotten to know her better."

Amy raised her eyebrows sarcastically. "And that's a good thing?"

Matt sighed. "Look, this isn't getting us anywhere." He looked at her. "I might be dating Ashley, but you're still one of my best friends, Amy. Don't ask me to choose between you — please."

Amy wavered. She hated the thought of Matt dating Ashley, but she couldn't bear the thought of losing him as a friend. "OK," she said at last. "I guess it really isn't my business who you go out with."

"So we're friends again?" Matt smiled.

Amy nodded. "Yeah, we're friends." She managed a teasing smile. "Even if you do have awful taste in girl-friends."

"Well, I did ask *you* out, didn't I?" Matt grinned.

Amy punched his arm and they walked toward the barn.

Reaching Daybreak and Melody's stall, they found the foal standing up, suckling vigorously. Scott and Marnie were watching.

"Hey, girl," said Amy, going into the stall.

"She's feeding. That's a good sign," Scott said.

Amy held the filly still while Scott checked her over.

"Yes, she's definitely on the mend," he said at last as he folded up his stethoscope. "Her breathing's improved, her temperature's almost back to normal, and her glands aren't as swollen. I think we can safely say she's over the worst."

Amy breathed out deeply in relief.

"Now, keep up the treatments and the nursing," Scott said. He glanced out the door. "She needs as much fresh air as possible. The wind's died down, so you can take her and Melody out for a gentle walk on the lead, but don't turn them out in the field until the weather improves. She's OK to go out in the snow for a while if it's sunny, but keep her out of wind and rain for now. She needs to stay warm and dry."

"Sure," Amy nodded.

Scott smiled at her. "You're doing a great job, Amy. Daybreak's very lucky to have you around."

Amy felt embarrassed by his words of praise. As they all walked back across the yard together, she changed the subject. "Has Lou called you yet?" she asked Scott as they reached the Jeep.

Scott nodded. "She called last night. She was pretty upset about your dad and everything."

"I know," Amy agreed. "I just hope she gets home soon."

Scott was silent for a moment. "Me, too," he said at last, and climbed into the driver's seat.

"See you, Amy," Matt said, opening the passenger door and getting in. "That is, if you ever decide to come back to school."

"Yeah," Amy said with a smile. "Say hi to Soraya, and tell her I'll call her tonight."

She felt hopeful as she watched them drive off. Things were somewhat back to normal with Matt, and Lou must have apologized when she'd called Scott. Amy couldn't really ask Scott. She knew her sister, and Lou was very strong — and also *very* stubborn. But Amy was certain she was missing Scott, or she wouldn't have phoned him. *Perhaps they've made up after all,* she thought.

Ty came down the yard. "So what did Scott say about Daybreak?"

"He's really pleased with her progress," Amy said. "He said we should walk her and Melody out in the yard this afternoon."

Ty raised his eyebrows. "That'll be fun. A loose foal is just what we need right now."

"Come on, she was getting better at leading before she got sick," Amy said hopefully. "She might not be that bad."

Ty didn't look convinced.

&

"So how are all the horses?" Grandpa asked when Amy and Marnie visited him at lunchtime.

"OK," Amy said, glad to be able to tell the truth for once.

"What about Lou?" Grandpa asked. "Has she seen your father yet?"

Amy hesitated. All the tubes and drips had been removed from Grandpa's body and he was starting to look much better. She decided it was best to tell him the truth. "No," she said. "It turns out that he's living in Australia."

"In Australia?" Grandpa echoed.

Amy nodded and told him everything.

"Oh, poor Lou," Grandpa said when she finished. "She must be so disappointed."

"She is," Amy said quietly. "It sounds like she feels the whole trip was a mistake."

"So when's she coming home?" Grandpa asked.

"As soon as possible," Amy replied. "There's a strike at the airport, but she's going to get the first flight out that she can."

Grandpa looked worried. "I hope she's back in time for Christmas."

"I know," Amy said. "I do, too."

✠

That afternoon Amy fetched Melody's and Daybreak's halters. "Now be good," she told Daybreak.

She haltered Melody and then approached Daybreak. To her surprise, the little filly stood quietly.

"Good girl," Amy praised Daybreak as she buckled up the halter and slipped the lead rope through the leather band. She rubbed the little foal's head. Daybreak looked at her and then lowered her nose.

"Are you ready?" Ty said, coming into the stall.

Amy nodded. Ty led Melody out, and clicking her tongue, Amy followed with Daybreak.

Daybreak's ears pricked as soon as Ty opened the door to the outside and the daylight streamed in. She surged slightly ahead of Amy. "Easy now," Amy said, checking her. As she did so, Amy tensed, half expecting Daybreak to explode with indignation. But to her surprise, the filly slowed down obediently. "Good girl," Amy praised, astonished.

They continued to walk around the yard without incident. It turned out to be a pleasant jaunt.

"She was great," Ty said when they put Daybreak and Melody back in their stall ten minutes later.

"I know," Amy said. "She didn't barge or push me or try to rear."

"She's probably still feeling too weak to put up a fight," Ty said.

Amy stared at the filly for a moment. She wasn't sure. She might have been imagining it, but out in the yard it had seemed to her that Daybreak hadn't *wanted* to fight anymore. She wondered whether to say anything to Ty and then decided not to. He was probably right. Daybreak was still recovering from a serious illness. No wonder she was being quiet.

❧

However, over the next few days, as Daybreak regained her strength, she also continued to behave. It was too windy for her and Melody to go out in the pasture, so twice a day Ty and Amy led the mare and her little foal around the yard. Not once did Daybreak show any sign of fighting the lead rope. And not only did she not fight it, she seemed willing to follow Amy on a loose rope wherever Amy wanted to go.

And it wasn't just the leading in the yard. Even in the stall, Amy noticed a change in Daybreak. Although the filly never whinnied to Amy like Melody did, she did whatever Amy asked without trying to resist.

By Friday, two days before Christmas, Amy was convinced that she wasn't imagining the change in the foal. "I'm sure she's getting better," she said to Ty as they brought Melody and Daybreak back to their stall after one of their yard walks. "Look." She stopped the foal with the lead rope and, by pressing on her sides, got her to move forward, sideways, and backward. Daybreak's eyes didn't even flicker. She moved where Amy wanted, responding to the lightest pressure from Amy's hands, her intelligent eyes calm. "She wouldn't have done that before she was sick," Amy said, patting her.

"You're right," Ty admitted. "There has been a change in her."

"Why do you think it's happened?" Amy asked.

"I don't know," Ty said. "Maybe it had something to do with the virus. Maybe she learned that she could trust you when you took care of her and helped her feel better."

An image came into Amy's mind of the night she had worked T-touch on Daybreak. She remembered how upset she had been and how massaging Daybreak had put her at ease. And she remembered, too, how the resentment in the foal's eyes had gradually faded as her fingers had worked on and on. Maybe the change in Daybreak had happened then. Maybe that feeling of peace had enveloped them both. Who could tell? She stroked the little foal. All that mattered was that Daybreak had come to respect and trust them and now she was willing to work with them.

She and Ty put the mare and foal back into their stall. As they came out of the barn Ty said, "Have you had any news from Lou?"

"She called last night," Amy replied. "The strike's still on." She swallowed. "It's beginning to look like Marnie and I might be having Christmas on our own."

Ty looked at her sympathetically. "Look, why don't I come over — spend the day here with you."

Amy smiled but shook her head. "Thanks, Ty, but your family will want to see you. You're here enough as it is."

"I don't mind," Ty said softly.

Amy's mind suddenly filled with the memory of his birthday. "Marnie and I will be fine," she managed, feeling a blush flooding into her cheeks.

Just then there was the sound of the phone ringing. "I'll get it," Amy said, relieved.

She ran to the kitchen and grabbed the receiver. "Hello, Heartland," she said.

"Hi, Amy, it's me."

"Grandpa!" Amy said with surprise. She felt suddenly worried. "Are you OK? There's nothing wrong, is there?"

"No," Grandpa said. "There's nothing wrong. In fact," Amy heard the smile in his voice, "there's something very right."

"What?" Amy asked.

"The hospital has told me I can come home, Amy. I'll be back for Christmas after all."

Chapter Thirteen

❧

Amy could hardly believe it. "But that's fabulous!" she gasped.

"I know." Grandpa sounded equally amazed. "I've had to promise to take it very easy, of course, and I need to come back for a checkup on the twenty-sixth, but at least I'll be with you for the holiday."

"So when can we come and get you?" Amy said.

"Anytime," Grandpa said.

"I can't wait to tell Marnie!" Amy exclaimed. Just then she saw Marnie's car pulling up outside. "Look, I'd better go," she said, wanting to tell her the good news about Grandpa. "We'll be over to get you in about an hour."

Putting the phone down, she ran outside. Marnie

grinned excitedly as she told her about her Grandpa's call. "That's wonderful news," she cried, hugging Amy.

"What is?" Ben said, turning off the water tap and heading over. "Did Lou get a flight?"

Amy shook her head. "Not yet. But Grandpa's coming home!"

"Oh, wow!" Ben exclaimed. "So you're not going to be on your own for Christmas after all?"

"No," Amy said, her eyes sparkling with happiness.

Ben smiled. "I was going to offer to stay."

Amy grinned. "Not you, too?"

Ben looked confused. "What?"

"It doesn't matter," Amy said. She hugged him. "But you and Ty are really the nicest guys!"

Amy set off with Marnie to the hospital. They went in Grandpa's car so there would be more room. When they got there, they found him already waiting, his bag packed.

"Now you take it easy, Mr. Bartlett," Dr. Marshall warned, coming to see him off. "And remember your antibiotics."

"I will," Grandpa smiled. "Thank you for everything, Doctor."

"No problem," she said with a smile. "And we'll see you right after the holiday for one final check."

"I can't believe you're really coming home, Grandpa," Amy said happily as they went to the car.

"No, I can't either," Grandpa said, smiling. "And it's Christmas Eve tomorrow!"

"I'm afraid we're not really in the Christmas spirit," Marnie said.

"The decoration boxes are still stacked in the hallway where you left them," Amy explained.

"Well, we'll soon see to that," Grandpa said.

"Grandpa! Were you even listening to the doctor? You've got to take it easy!" Amy protested.

"Oh, I'm planning to take it easy," Grandpa said, coughing slightly. "But that doesn't mean I can't organize *you* two."

On the way home, he made them stop and buy the biggest Christmas tree they could find.

"I'm glad we brought your car," Marnie said, easing into the driver's seat after she and Amy had securely strapped the tree to the roof.

"We can't have Christmas without a tree," Grandpa said.

When they got back, they found that they hadn't been the only ones thinking about Christmas. Ty and Ben had found the battered boxes of old decorations in the hall and had set to work making the yard and the house look as festive as possible. Fairy lights flickered along the roof of the front stable, and the kitchen, porch, and tack room had been decorated with Christmas garlands.

"Oh, cool!" Amy said, jumping out of the car.

Ty and Ben came down the yard.

"Welcome home, Jack," Ty said, helping Grandpa out of the car. "It's great to have you back."

Grandpa looked around, a contented smile on his face. "It's good to *be* back," he said.

With Grandpa back at Heartland, the whole house came alive again. He spent the evening supervising Amy and Marnie as they decorated the Christmas tree and put up all the cards that had arrived. Amy tried to call her sister to tell her that Grandpa was home, but when she spoke to the hotel, they said that Ms. Fleming had checked out several hours earlier. Knowing that Lou had been planning to stay with friends if she didn't get a flight home that day, Amy wasn't too worried. She just wanted to tell her the good news.

Later that evening, the phone rang. Amy raced to answer it but it wasn't Lou. It was Soraya. "Have you had any news from Lou?" she asked.

"No," Amy replied, "but Grandpa's home from the hospital. They discharged him early."

"That's great!" Soraya said.

"I know. I just wish Lou was going to be here, too. We'll just have to celebrate again when she gets home," Amy said. She sighed and then changed the subject. "So, are you coming over tomorrow?"

Every Christmas Eve Soraya came over to help with the horses and they went out for a long trail ride in the afternoon after the chores were done.

"Of course," Soraya said. "I'll come just after nine."

"Great," Amy said, pleased. "I'll see you then."

❧

When Amy woke up the next morning she became aware of a change in the air. She went to the window. There had been another fall of snow overnight. A heavy white blanket covered the fields and trees and everything was quiet and still. The chill wind that had been blowing for the last week or so had finally died down.

Amy pulled on her clothes and went downstairs. Both Grandpa and Marnie were still in bed. Taking a few cookies from the tin on the shelf, she went outside and stood for a moment in the quiet world. *It's Christmas Eve,* she thought, a pleasant tingle of anticipation running down her spine.

Ty and Ben arrived an hour later at seven o'clock, and they all set to work on the horses. They were mucking out when Marnie came outside with coffee for everyone.

"I'm going to cook a huge brunch," she announced, handing Ty and Ben insulated mugs. She grinned at Amy. "It's the only way I can stop your grandpa from doing it."

"Thanks," Amy said gratefully, blowing on her steaming coffee.

"No problem," Marnie replied. "It'll be ready about ten."

❧

Amy forked the last few pieces of dirty straw from Jake's stall into the wheelbarrow. She was so glad that Grandpa was home for Christmas. *If only Lou were here, too,* she thought, *then everything really would be perfect.*

She had just emptied the wheelbarrow when she heard the sound of a car engine. Thinking it would be Soraya, she ran outside. To her surprise, she saw Scott driving up.

"Hey," Scott said as he got out of his Jeep. "I - wasn't doing anything this morning so I thought I'd drop by and see if you could use some help with the horses."

"That's really nice of you," Amy said, touched at the gesture.

"How's your grandpa?" Scott asked.

"He's better. In fact, he's here," Amy said, realizing that Scott wouldn't have heard the news. "We brought him home last night."

"That's wonderful!" Scott exclaimed. "Is he well enough for me to go in and say hello?"

"I guess so." Amy thought about the way Grandpa had been bossing her and Marnie around the night before and smiled. "He'd love to see you."

Scott went down to the house.

Amy had just started on Sundance's stall when Soraya arrived. She jumped out of her mom's car almost before it had stopped. "Hi!" she said, hugging Amy. "How are you?"

"Great," Amy said, and she really meant it.

℞

With Scott and Soraya helping, the mucking out took no time at all. As Amy was finishing Moochie's stall she realized that the clouds overhead had parted and blue sky was showing through.

She went into the next stall where Ty was grooming Jake. "Do you think the wind's calm enough to turn out Melody and Daybreak for a while?"

"Yeah, definitely," Ty said, glancing out of the stall. "Do you want a hand?"

"Thanks," Amy said gratefully.

They got the mare and foal and led them out through the snow to the paddock beside the house. Daybreak looked around excitedly, her nostrils flaring as she breathed in the crisp, clear air. Despite her eagerness to be out in the field, she walked obediently beside Amy.

"She's so much better," Ty said, looking at her.

"Yeah." Amy grinned happily. "She's a little lady now."

They reached the field gate and unclipped the lead ropes. With a loud snort, Daybreak trotted out across the snowy grass.

In the center of the field she stopped, her beautiful head held high, the tips of her tiny ears almost meeting. For a moment she stood poised and statuelike, every muscle tense. Then, with a sudden toss of her head, she squealed mischievously and plunged forward in a blur of glowing chestnut, her back legs kicking up a clump of snowflakes.

Amy's heart swelled with happiness. The little filly might submit willingly to a halter and lead rope now, but her spirit was far from broken. She was still fiery, proud, and free.

Wheeling around, Daybreak cantered toward the gate. Amy expected to see her go over to Melody. Instead, she trotted slowly past her mother, stopped, and looked at Amy.

Very slowly, wondering what she wanted, Amy stepped into the field and held out her hand. "Here, girl," she said softly.

Daybreak hesitated and then, with the faintest of whickers, she walked forward. Stretching her head forward, she nuzzled Amy's upturned palm. Then, lifting her tiny muzzle to Amy's face, she breathed out warmly, love and trust glowing in her dark eyes.

Amy was filled with triumph and delight. Daybreak's fight was over. Suddenly, all the frustration and sleepless nights that the foal had caused her were forgotten. Breathing in the sweet scent of Daybreak's breath, she kissed the little filly's nose.

"Daybreak," she whispered softly. "My Daybreak."

The moment was shattered by the sound of the back door opening and Marnie calling out, "Brunch is ready, everyone!"

With a swift toss of her head, Daybreak plunged away.

Amy turned and met Ty's eyes.

"I can hardly believe it, Amy," he said softly. "You've won her trust."

Amy's face glowed as she went over to the gate. "We did it together," she said, knowing that she could never have done it without him.

He smiled at her and they headed to the house.

&

The kitchen table was piled high with food. There were dishes of crispy bacon, grilled sausages, and golden scrambled eggs, two huge bowls of fresh fruit salad, a platter of steaming blueberry pancakes, two pitchers of maple syrup, and a mountain of freshly baked muffins and cinnamon rolls.

"Sit down, everyone," Marnie said as they all kicked off their boots.

"Wow!" Ben said, looking around. "This is some spread."

Grandpa was sitting at the head of the table. "Who wants coffee?"

"I'll do that, Jack," said Scott, taking the coffeepot from him. "You just sit there and enjoy."

Talking and laughing, everybody pulled chairs up to the table.

"This is incredible, Marnie," Amy said, carrying a pile of warmed plates to the table.

"Thanks," she replied. "Jack instructed me from the armchair!"

Amy put the plates down on the table. "Now, everyone help themselves," she said, handing them out.

She had just sat down between Ty and Soraya when the back door opened.

Amy jumped to her feet and turned around. "Lou!" she exclaimed.

A silence fell on the room. Lou stood in the doorway. Her hair was disheveled and her face was tired. She was looking around in astonishment at the crowded kitchen.

"What's — what's going on?" Suddenly, her eyes fell on Grandpa. "Grandpa!" she gasped. "You're home!"

Dropping her bag, she rushed over to him. He rose to meet her. "Oh, Lou, it's so good to see you! We weren't expecting you for ages."

"I got a flight!" Lou said. "The strike was suddenly called off. I couldn't call. There was no time. As soon as I found out I could get a seat I had to get on that plane and come home," she said, pulling back from him with a relieved smile. "I still can't believe it. And to get here and find you home, Grandpa! I thought you'd still be in the hospital."

"They released me yesterday," Grandpa said.

"On strict instructions that he take it easy," smiled Amy, butting in.

"I've been so worried about you!" Lou exclaimed. "Leaving here while you were so ill was the stupidest thing I could have done. I don't know what I was thinking."

"But I made you go, Lou," Grandpa said, reaching for her hand. "I thought it was something you needed to do."

"You knew how important it was to me," Lou said sadly. "I *thought* I needed to go, too, but being away from here and away from all of you helped me figure things out." She sighed deeply. "I was just too focused on finding Daddy. I was blind to everything else. Please forgive me."

Jack smiled. "There's nothing to forgive," he said.

"But there is," Lou insisted. "I was really selfish." She turned to her sister. "I should have been here to help while Grandpa was sick instead of running off to London. It must have been really hard on you. I'm so sorry, Amy."

"It doesn't matter anymore," Amy said, hugging her in delight. "I'm just glad you're back."

"You're don't know how glad I am to *be* back. Being away made me realize a lot of things." Lou paused. "I can't go on searching for my father anymore. I know that's a mistake — we'll meet up soon enough. I don't need to put my life on hold waiting for him. There are more important things for me here." Lou smiled and looked across the room at Scott.

She walked over to him. "Scott, I need to apologize to you, too. I'm sorry I missed your dinner, and I'm sorry I couldn't see your side of things. I didn't mean to —"

Before Lou could finish apologizing, Scott wrapped his arms around her. "It doesn't matter, Lou. I know you didn't mean it. I missed you so much."

"I've missed you, too," Lou said, half laughing, half crying. "I'll make it up to everyone, I promise."

Amy sank down in her chair, her legs feeling suddenly shaky. Lou was back. Now *everyone* was home for Christmas.

Just then the phone rang. Marnie picked it up. "Hello, Heartland."

She looked at Lou, frowning. "Lou," she said. Amy couldn't help noticing a strange tone in her voice. "It's for you."

"Can you tell them I'll call back?" Lou said, turning happily in Scott's arms.

"Well — it's a long distance call," Marnie said. "It's — from Australia."

Lou's face suddenly paled. "Australia?" she whispered.

Marnie nodded. "It's your father."

"You don't have to talk to him, Lou," Amy said quickly. "You —"

But Lou had already pulled away from Scott and taken the phone. "Hello," she said, her voice catching in her throat. "Daddy?"

Turning, she walked out of the room and into the hall. She shut the door behind her.

No one spoke. Amy looked at Grandpa. His face was tense.

After about five minutes, the door opened and Lou came back in. Amy's eyes flew to her sister's face. She was even paler and her blue eyes looked shocked. She handed the receiver to Amy. "He — he wants to speak to you," she said, her voice now low and shaky.

Amy shook her head frantically, but Lou shoved the

receiver in her hand and walked away to the sink. For a moment Amy didn't know what to do, but then very slowly, she lifted the phone to her ear. "Hello?" she whispered, turning away from everyone in the room.

"Hello, Amy." The strange English voice on the other end of the line seemed unfamiliar at first, but deep in the corners of Amy's mind a long-forgotten memory stirred. She wanted to speak but just couldn't.

"I guess you don't remember me that well."

"No," Amy said, her heart beating fast.

"Well, I remember you," her father said, his voice warm. "In fact, I've got a photo of you in my wallet. You and Lou at the seaside. I carry it with me all the time."

Amy didn't know what to say. For twelve years her father had been absent from her life, and now suddenly, here he was, talking to her on the telephone.

Her father seemed to feel the awkwardness of the situation, too. "Look, I'm sorry for calling out of the blue like this," he said. "I wanted to meet you face-to-face after all this time, but when I heard from the Carters that Lou had been to England to find me, I knew that I had to call and explain."

Amy was silent.

"I live on a large farm here," her father went on. "I raise horses. Lou said in her letter that you're really into horses. You'd like it here."

Amy didn't say anything. Suddenly, she heard the sound of crying in the background. "Is that a baby?" she asked.

"Yes," her father said. There was a pause. "My wife gave birth to our little girl last week."

For a moment the world seemed to stop. The words ran through Amy's head. *Wife. Baby.* She looked at Lou's back and suddenly she understood the shocked look she had just seen in her sister's eyes.

"I just explained to Lou that's why I can't meet you until February," their father continued. "I need to be here at the moment. It's also why I didn't tell you that I'm living in Australia. I thought the news that I'd remarried and that you had a half sister might be better if I told you in person."

"I understand," Amy whispered.

There was a silence.

"Look, I think I'd better give you a little time to let all this news sink in," her father said. "There's much more that we need to talk about, but that can wait. I'll call again after the holidays, if that's OK. For now, let me just wish you a merry Christmas, Amy, and I look forward to seeing you in the new year."

"O — OK," Amy stammered. "Bye, Daddy."

As Amy put the phone down, Lou turned and met her eyes. Her face was wet with tears.

"What did he say?" Grandpa asked, looking anxious.

Amy looked around, her head spinning. "That he's married and they've just had a baby girl."

She saw the shock register on everyone's face.

"A baby!" Grandpa echoed. He stood up, his face suddenly dour. "Lou —"

"I'm all right," Lou interrupted. She lifted her head and brushed the tears away from her eyes. "I'm — I'm *glad* that Daddy's found some happiness at last."

"Do you mean that?" Grandpa said.

"Yes," Lou replied, going to Scott's side and taking his hand. "Daddy's got his life now, and I've got mine. And it's here at Heartland with all of you." Tears still glistened in her eyes, but she smiled and took a deep breath. "I don't know about everyone else, but I'm starving," she said. "Are any of those eggs for me?"

It didn't take long to reheat the food. Soon everyone was sitting down, passing the dishes around, and eating heartily. As the noise level rose Amy thought about everything that had happened in the last six months. There had been so much grief, so much pain, and so many tears.

But not everything that had happened had been bad, she thought, looking at Ben and Marnie laughing with

Soraya. New friends had been made, old friendships strengthened. *And not just friendships*, she thought, her eyes looking to Lou. For so much of her life, her sister had been almost a stranger to her, but over the last six months a new bond had been forged between them. Now they didn't just love each other, they understood and needed each other, too.

As she finished the last piece of muffin on her plate, Ty nudged her with his elbow. "We should probably bring Melody and Daybreak in. We don't want Daybreak to be out too long."

Amy nodded and they stood up.

"You're not going back out already, are you?" Lou said to them. "I was just going to make some fresh coffee."

"We'll be back soon," Amy replied, smiling at her big sister. "We're just going to bring Melody and Daybreak in from the field."

She and Ty pulled on their boots and left the warmth of the house. After the laughter and noise of the kitchen, the stables held a soothing silence for them both. Only the occasional snort of one of the horses in the stalls broke the calm.

"Look," Ty said, pointing to the field.

Amy smiled. Melody and Daybreak were standing by the water trough. The foal was suckling, her fluffy tail switching from side to side as Melody gently nuzzled her hindquarters. The rays of the winter sun shone down on their backs.

Amy and Ty stopped by the gate.

"Everything seems so peaceful," Ty said.

Amy nodded and leaned against the gate. "It's so quiet," she said softly. "It makes it easy to forget all the craziness we've been through."

Ty's eyes met hers. "It's been a tough six months, Amy."

"Yeah — but it's been good, too," Amy said. "Lou's come back to live here, Grandpa's on the mend, Heartland's doing well, and I know how lucky I am to have my friends and family." She looked up at Ty, knowing he'd understand. "I still miss Mom and Pegasus — I always will — but it's time to move on." She paused for a moment and watched the mare and filly in the field. When she spoke again, her voice was quiet. "You remember how Mom used to say, 'One day you'll know when the good times are here'?"

Ty nodded.

"Well, I had some wonderful times *with* Mom," Amy said slowly. "But now I know I've got to find my own good times, too. It's what Mom would have wanted."

"You're right," Ty said softly. "It is."

Amy met his gaze. She didn't know what she'd have

done without him over the last six months. "Thank you," she said suddenly.

"For what?" Ty asked, looking surprised.

"For being here," Amy said. "For helping me." She saw him about to speak, to shrug it off, but she shook her head, wanting to tell him just how much he meant to her. "If it hadn't been for you, Ty, Heartland wouldn't even exist anymore. You're very important to Heartland — and to me."

"And you're important to me," Ty said warmly. He stepped closer.

Amy felt her stomach somersault as she looked up at him. "Ty?" she said as his hands touched her shoulders.

But Ty didn't speak. His eyes looked deep into hers and then his lips met her own.

Amy didn't know how long the kiss lasted. But when it stopped, her heart was pounding so hard she thought it was going to burst. "Ty?" she stammered.

Ty looked down at her and smiled. "Merry Christmas, Amy," he said. "I hope the good times come soon."

Amy glanced at Melody and Daybreak, then around at the house. Through the kitchen windows, with their festive decorations, she could see everyone she loved most in the world gathered together. "I think they're here already," she said, looking back at Ty. "They really are."

As she opened the field gate Daybreak whinnied, and with a smile, Amy walked across the snow toward the little foal.